MR. DIAZ'S
REVENGE

D.W. ULSTERMAN

D.W. ULSTERMAN

CHAPTER 1

7:52 a.m.

It was a Monday, the beginning of another long week. It was also the day the bastards were finally going to get what was coming to them.

A day for revenge.

A day for death.

Normally, Mr. Amos Diaz hated Mondays during the school year. Mondays meant morning staff meetings and another four work days before the far too brief reprieve of the weekend.

This Monday would be different.

This Monday, Mr. Diaz brought a gun.

It was inside the briefcase on the passenger seat of his shitty little 1997 Honda, hidden beneath a stack of equally shitty essays he had been ignoring for weeks. Only a few students had bothered to ask him when they would be graded. The rest didn't care.

Amos adjusted the rearview mirror. His sleep-deprived eyes stared back at him. He had been too nervous to rest. Too hopeful everything would soon be over. No more humiliation. No more pretending. No more regret. No more anything.

The anticipation was killing him. He faked a smile, laughed at himself, rubbed his eyes, shook his head, and looked away. The first period bell sounded across the parking lot.

School was in session.

Amos had first period prep. That meant no students and plenty of time to prepare. He grabbed the briefcase and got out of the car.

"Late again, Mr. Diaz."

Principal Doyle Dardner's tapioca pudding face was the perfect complement to his perpetually talking-down-to-you tone. "I'm not late," Amos replied. "I was in my car."

Dardner adjusted his glasses, shook his oversized potato head, and then crinkled his nose like he'd just stepped in dog shit. "I won't even bother to mention the missed staff meeting," he said. "What if you had a student who wanted to see you before class? How are they supposed to do that if you're hiding in your car? You know the rules. Teachers are to be available to students from 7:35 a.m. to 3:15 p.m. every school day. Why is it you seem to think you're the exception?"

"I don't."

"Really? And yet here you are getting out of your vehicle after the first period bell."

Amos started to walk across the strip of grass separating the staff parking lot and the building where his classroom was located. Students moved back and forth along the sidewalk some forty feet from where Dardner stood. One of them, a senior boy, shouted at a freshman about how he was going to make her kiss the hog in his pants.

Dardner cleared his throat. "I'm not done talking to you."

Amos whirled around. He gripped the briefcase so tightly his dark knuckles went white.

"You have something you'd like to say to me, Mr. Diaz?"

The answer squeezed out between Amos's tightly clenched teeth. "No."

"We need a cover in the library. Ms. Moore is out with the flu."

"I can't. I have papers to grade."

"You can grade them in the library."

"You'll have to get someone else. I'm sorry."

Dardner crossed his little alligator-like arms over his narrow, sunken chest. "We don't have anyone else. I need you to get to the library right now. I'm not asking."

"Just keep it closed for the day."

"What? The library?"

"Yeah. I can't do it. I have too much work."

The freshman girl cried out as the senior boy pinched her butt while some other male students laughed. "I already told you I'm not asking," Dardner said.

The girl cried out again. Another boy was holding her arms while the first one fondled her small breasts and licked his lips.

"You find this funny, Mr. Diaz?"

"As a matter of fact, I do."

"Are you refusing my request?"

"You tell me."

Dardner scowled. "What's wrong with you? All I'm

asking is for you to cover the library first period. We can't have students in there unsupervised. It's a liability issue."

"Why can't you do it?"

The corners of Dardner's mouth twitched. "I'm the principal. I have a school to run. I can't be everywhere at once."

"I'm a teacher. I have classes to prepare. First period is when I do that."

"Get to the library. That's an order."

"I'm sorry. Are we in the military?"

Dardner ran a hand across his thin-haired scalp as his face turned various shades of red. "Goddammit, Amos, am I going to have to write you up again? This will be the third time. I know you know what that means."

"Third time? No. Remind me."

"It means it would be an actionable offense. I could suspend you."

"Like a vacation? With pay? Do tell."

The girl tried to escape. The circle of boys around her closed in.

"I'm serious, Mr. Diaz."

"You might want to do something about the harassment going on behind you, Principal Dardner. I'm pretty sure that's against the rules outlined in the handbook you made sure were given to all the students at the beginning of the year."

"I can have Officer Markley escort you off campus right before I call the superintendent and file a formal insubordination complaint."

Sixty-four-year-old Rory Markley was a retired

cop who had accepted a position last year as the school district's only resource officer. Amos only knew the name. He hadn't met him. Like most district administrators, Markley seemed to prefer hanging out inside his office with the door closed.

"That won't be necessary."

Dardner smirked. "I didn't think so. Now if you could make your way to the library, I'd appreciate it."

The female student shouted to be left alone. One of the boys filmed her increasingly fearful reaction with his phone while laughing at her. Dardner walked away without looking back, leaving the girl to fend for herself.

"Hey," Amos shouted. "Let the young lady get to class." The boys continued to put their hands on her. She started to cry.

Amos unlatched the briefcase. "I said let her go."

A boy left. Then another. And then another until only the girl and the first boy remained. He held her by the arm.

"Take your hand off her," Amos said.

"Or what? You gonna throw your suitcase at me?"

"It's a briefcase not a suitcase."

The student rolled his eyes. "Like I care. Fuck off. Don't you have a library to get to?"

"What's your name?"

"My name is suck my dick."

Amos opened the briefcase a few inches. "I'm only going to ask you one more time. Let her get to class."

The girl pulled free and walked away while Mr. Suck My Dick glared at Amos. "There," he sneered. "I let her go."

"Thank you. Now you get to class as well."

"Fucking teachers. You're all losers."

Amos latched the briefcase closed. "Yeah."

"See? Even you agree. This place is a dumpster fire."

"Then why do you come here?"

The student shrugged. "I don't know. Why do you?"

"I'm paid to be here."

"Pfft, teachers don't get paid. Not real money anyways. You all live off cat food and shit. Everybody knows that."

Amos started to walk. "Don't knock it until you try it."

"What?"

"Cat food. Some of those flavors are pretty good. I'm partial to the chopped liver."

"You're crazy."

Amos stopped. "Hey, where's your first period class?"

"None of your business."

"Actually, it is. I can call in to the office and find out."

"Then why are you asking me?"

"It'd be easier if you'd just tell me."

"And why would I do that?"

"Do what?"

The student's eyes narrowed. "Are you retarded?"

"Maybe. So, about that first period."

"Good luck calling the office. You don't even know my name."

Amos looked the student up and down. "Skinny,

white, about six foot. Oversized black puffy jacket. Shoes with the toes nearly rotted out. A dirty blonde strip mall haircut and a sad attempt to grow a mustache. I think the office staff will manage to pull your name up pretty quick."

"I'm not white. I don't hold myself down to just one color. That's racist. You should know better."

"And why's that?"

"Because, you know, you're Mexican or something."

Amos shook his head. "I'm not Mexican. My father was Cuban and my mother African American."

"Mexican, Cuban, African, who gives a shit. It's all the same, right?"

"No, not really."

"I bet that's how you got your job here. Because you're Mexican? Part of that diversity quota bullshit? You said it yourself. You're a retard. Why else would they hire you?"

Amos sighed. "I guess you have all the answers, don't you?"

"Fucking right, I do."

"Mr. Diaz, what are you still doing out here? I thought I made it clear you were to be in the library." Dardner had returned.

The student flashed his middle finger in front of Amos's face. "Busted, asshole."

"I was trying to get this young man to report to his first period class," Amos replied. "He wasn't cooperating."

"Did I ask you to do that? No, I did not. What I did ask was that you cover the library first period, which started nearly five minutes ago, yet here you are, not doing what I requested, and then using a student as an excuse."

"Are you going to be in your office later this morning after announcements?"

Dardner scowled. "What?"

"I think I'll stop by and pay you a visit."

"Is that some kind of threat?"

"That's right," the student said while snapping his fingers. "He threatened me too. Teachers can't be doing that shit. It's against the Constitution."

Dardner pointed at the student while looking at Amos. "Is that true? Did you threaten Randal?"

Randal shook his head while grimacing. "Ah, man, now he knows my name."

"No," Amos answered.

"You sure about that?"

"Yeah."

Dardner turned to Randal. "Who do you have first period with, Mr. Risen?"

Amos chuckled. "Randal Risen, huh? That's quite a name."

"Shit," Randal said. "Now he knows my full name. That's like endangerment or something. I'm gonna sue this goddamn place."

Dardner adjusted his glasses. "You're a senior, right? I'm guessing you have Mrs. Hurst. Well, if she tries to give you a tardy, you tell her to come talk to me and I'll clear it up for you, okay?"

Randal rolled his head from one shoulder to the other. "Yeah, I'll tell her what's up. And you also need to keep this fag teacher off my ass. I don't like how he

8

looks at me. He keeps doing it, I'm gonna mess him up. I mean it."

"That's fine, Randal. I understand. Now please get to first period. Thank you."

Dardner watched Randal leave and then turned to Amos. "You see? That's how you diffuse a situation, Mr. Diaz. That's how you get students back into a learning environment. Not by threatening them but by reasoning with them. They're not animals."

Amos's eyes were burning ice. "I'll see you soon, Mr. Dardner."

"In my office?"

Amos turned around. "That's right."

"What about?"

"Just be there."

"I might stop by the library first to check in on you."

"Fine. I'll be waiting."

"For what?"

"For you," Amos answered with a smile.

CHAPTER 2

8:04 a.m.

The library was already unlocked but empty. Amos turned on the lights and went to the back office. He dropped his briefcase on the desk, started a pot of coffee, and looked out at the rows of alphabetized books that ran the length of the large room.

He collapsed into the chair next to the desk and leaned back until the top of his head touched the concrete wall behind him. He sat like that for a while listening to the coffee machine groaning like an old man getting out of bed.

A door opened. Julia Hodson walked in and smiled.

"Hey, Amos. What are you doing here?"

"Covering for Ms. Moore. Dardner said she's out sick."

Most everyone at the school liked Julia. She taught art. At thirty-nine, she was ten years younger than Amos. Her spikey blonde hair and lean, athletic body were a perfect complement to her wide, white smile, which she flashed often throughout the school day. Unlike most of the other teaching inmates, she loved her job.

"Were you looking for her?"

Julia nodded. "Yeah. I have first period prep. I come in here sometimes to grab a decent cup of coffee. The sludge in the faculty lounge is barely tolerable." She looked around. "I see the library is its usual abandoned self."

"It's normally like this?"

"Uh-huh. I don't think kids read books anymore. They used to come in here for the computers but now those are pretty much obsolete as well. All they care to know about is on their phones, so why would they bother stopping by here? Ronda's actually worried the district is going to keep slashing her budget. She seems worried about a lot of things lately. I try to cheer her up, but I also know she's probably right."

Amos grunted. "Huh. I sure hope that's not true. Libraries are one of the few things left that still seem...civilized. They help to make us more human."

"Why, Mr. Diaz, you almost sound like a romantic."

"No, just a little nostalgic I suppose."

"There's nothing wrong with that. Hey, do I smell fresh coffee?"

"You want some?"

"That would be great. Thanks."

Amos poured a cup for each of them. Julia took a sip from hers and smiled. "Not bad. I wonder why Dardner made you cover for Ronda when he knows I come in here all the time during my prep anyways?"

"Because he's an asshole."

"I won't argue that. He'll wander around the halls a little when classes are in session, but I've seen him repeatedly scurry back into his office right before the bell rings. It's like the students terrify him or something. Makes you wonder why he ever got into education in the first place. I take it you two don't get along?"

"I don't respect him. Never have."

"You ever consider teaching somewhere else?"

"Not really. Bad administrators are everywhere. You can't outrun them. The whole system is, for lack of a better term, screwed."

"Hmmm, from romantic to depressed. You're an extremist."

"No, I'm a realist. I know you like it here. I envy that. Me? I just see failure, hopelessness, kids lost, teachers who've given up, and incompetent administrators who never cared. Isn't it strange how in our profession, the farther you get from actually interacting with students, the more money you make? What's your salary this year? Fifty thousand? Sixty? Do you know the superintendent who sits in a space at the district office that's about the size of this entire library makes nearly $180k?"

Julia's mouth fell open. "Dr. Miller makes that much? Wow. Well, good for him I guess."

"He makes that much and the two other assistant superintendents the district hired on also make close to the same. Then there's the administrative assistants, we have four of those, the curriculum development coordinator, the student outreach office, the district counseling services administrator—it goes on and on. All that for a small district of about two thousand students. When I first started teaching, it wasn't like this. More money was going directly to the kids. Now? I'd wager less than ten cents of every operational dollar a district like this spends goes to students. And we wonder why everything is so messed up. Why kids don't care, parents don't care, teachers don't care. Nobody cares."

"I do."

Amos shrugged. "You're the exception. The rest of us? We're just marking time."

"That sounds awfully negative. So, you've given up?"

"More like given in."

"Is it really that bad?"

"For me? Yeah. I hate this place – every inch of it. Hate nearly every face – present company excluded."

"Thanks."

"Sure."

Julia touched Amos's arm. "Are you going to be okay?"

Amos sipped his coffee. "After today I might. Every day is a new ending, right?"

"Don't you mean a new beginning?"

"Is there a difference?"

"I'd like to think so. A big one. What's happening today?"

"Huh?"

"You said it was a new ending. You have something planned?"

Amos looked down at his coffee cup. "Uh, no, it was just a figure of speech."

"But you said you might be okay after today, which means you're not okay right now. What's wrong?"

"Nothing. I should be getting to work. I have papers to grade."

"You sure? If you need someone to talk to, I'm happy to—"

"No," Amos said while stepping back from the counter. "I'm fine. Really. Thanks."

"You mind if I stop by again before first period is over? I'd love a second cup of this coffee."

"I don't think I'll have time to talk."

Julia looked around at the empty library. "Really?"

"Sorry."

"You sure you're okay?"

Amos let out a nervous chuckle. "Sure. Why?"

"I don't know. This job can get to you. Anyone who's done it for more than a few years realizes that. Teachers need to look out for one another."

"Is that what you're doing? Looking out for me?"

Julia smiled. "No. I'm just here for the coffee. You take care, Mr. Diaz."

"You too, Ms. Hodson."

Right before Julia reached the door, Amos called out to her. "Are you going back to your room?"

"Yeah. Why?"

"Just wanted to know."

Julia's eyes narrowed. She took a few steps toward Amos while staring at him intently. "Is this about Stacy?"

Hearing the name out loud made Amos flinch. He shook his head. "No."

"How long were you two married?"

"Long enough that I don't want to talk about it."

Julia held up her hand and nodded. "Okay, I get it. I'm being nosey. You wouldn't be the first to accuse me of that. Still, if you decide later you do want to talk about it, my door is always open."

"Thanks, but that won't be necessary. You'll want to stay in your classroom this morning, Ms. Hodson."

"Uh, sure. That's where I'm headed now."

Amos lowered his head and stared at Julia. "That would be best."

Julia backed away slowly while keeping her eyes on Amos. She reached for the door behind her and pulled it open.

Amos was once again alone. He glanced at the digital red clock on the wall above the exit. Directly to the right of the door was the fire alarm.

It was almost time.

Amos went into the office, opened the briefcase, and took out the gun. It was an old Glock he had inherited years ago from his father. Amos had kept it in a shoebox on the top shelf of his bedroom closet where it had remained until this morning. He had never fired it. His father had belonged to a shooting club and the Glock was his weapon of choice for as long as Amos could remember. When fully loaded, as it was this morning, it held fifteen rounds and another in the chamber.

Fifteen and one.

More than enough to do what Amos knew needed to be done.

He would never want to kill them all. That would be wrong. He'd kill just enough to make people pay attention. To make a point. To get his message out.

Amos had something to say and today, he would say it, and nobody was going to stop him. Not Dardner. Not that little shit Randal Risen. Nobody.

Amos gripped the gun and held it out in front of him. It felt good. It felt right.

The library door opened. "Hello? You in here, Mr. Diaz?"

The man was older and of average height and build with white hair and a prominent paunch. He wore a uniform. Amos nearly dropped the Glock as he lowered it in a panic. He put it on the desk and covered it with a copy of The Catcher in the Rye.

The man smiled. "Ah, there you are. Sorry to startle you. I don't think we've ever actually met. I'm Officer Markley."

Amos walked out of the office. Rory stood on the other side of the counter with his hand extended. The two men shook.

"What can I do for you, Officer Markley?"

"Principal Dardner asked that I stop by to make sure you were here."

"I see."

"Yeah."

"Is that it?"

"Sure, here you are. I'll let him know. I also thought it'd be nice to put a face to the name. Seems I spend most my time working at the middle school. Those little monsters keep you on your toes, I'll tell you that. I've been here almost a year and haven't met everyone yet, so I'm glad to be able to cross you off that list."

Amos pointed to the wide belt around Rory's

ample waist. "You're not armed."

Markley glanced down and scowled. "No, when the position was created, the district decided to make me an unarmed resource officer. Some parents raised concerns about my presence creating a prison-like environment. I guess they thought it best I keep the kids in line with just my sunny disposition."

"How's that working out?"

"It's okay, I guess. I carried a gun on the job for a lot of years, so I'd be lying if I said I didn't miss the sense of security a sidearm brings, but the job pays on time every time, so I'm not complaining. Though, there are days like yesterday when it doesn't pay near enough."

"What happened yesterday?"

Rory leaned forward. "You didn't hear? I figured the whole district would have been talking about it. Had one heck of a dustup with a certain family who doesn't take kindly to being told what to do."

"What family?"

"You've been teaching here a while, right?"

"Yes."

"Then I'm sure you know all about the Burkes."

"Sure. I taught Willy Burke until he dropped out. That must have been, oh, twenty years ago."

"You know his son Walter?"

Amos shook his head. "I've heard of him, but he's never been a student of mine."

"Count yourself lucky. Walter is every bit as bad as his father when it comes to being a pain in the ass. Those two are fearlessly stupid. Anyways, Walter was suspended yesterday for the rest of the year for breaking some poor kid's face open. He really laid a whooping on him. I'm sure there'll be charges filed over it. I've called the police on Walter no fewer than seven times since I took this job. Seven times! So, his dad shows up here yesterday to pick Walter up, and Mr. Burke starts screaming at anyone and everyone about how his son was only doing what was right and that they'd both be back to burn the whole school down and everyone in it."

"Geez."

"Yeah. He was hollering and pointing all the way to his truck. Thank God the police were here to make sure he left without further incident. Had me shook up a bit. I've seen plenty during my time as a cop and I tell you what, those Burkes are trouble. That's why I was here this morning. Just wanted to make sure they didn't make good on their promise to come back. There was a shine to Willy Burke's eyes I didn't like one bit."

"Shine?"

"It's what cops call the amphetamine glow. The eyes get all lit up from the inside. Maybe it's meth, or pills, or anything and everything he can get his hands on, but Willy Burke was all cranked up on something, and given his known inclination toward violence, that's like pouring gasoline on an already out-of-control fire."

Markley's phone rang. "Hello? Uh-huh. Okay, I'll be right there." He put the phone away. "That," he said, "is yet another situation at the middle school. A trash fire or something. Funny how I had just mentioned fire right before that call. These damn kids. Am I right?" He again extended his hand across the counter. "It was good meeting you, Mr. Diaz. Sorry to talk your ear off. I live alone so don't get much chance to share what happens on this job. Guess I needed to unload. I'll let Principal Dardner know on my way out that you're here."

"Thanks," Amos said. "So, he's in his office?"

"Yeah, I'd assume so. Say, are you feeling okay? You're sweating."

Amos wiped his forehead. "Guess I should turn the heat down."

"You must be coming down with something because it's actually a little cold in here."

"Huh. I don't know. Probably just the coffee."

Rory stood looking at Amos. Then his phone rang again. "I have to go. Have a good one, Mr. Diaz."

"You too, Officer Markley."

After the door closed, Amos's shoulders slumped. His heart banged against his chest. He turned around, went into the office, and grabbed the gun. The unexpected visit from Markley had put him behind schedule. He jammed the Glock into the back of his slacks, walked toward the fire alarm, and then stopped and stared at the little red lever with the white letters that spelled out ALARM.

Amos took a deep breath and reached out to pull the lever.

The alarm's deep, wonk-wonk sound echoed off the library walls. Amos's hand drew back like it had been singed. He leaned forward. The lever remained untouched. He hadn't pulled it. Students walked by the library door. They were talking. Laughing. Being kids. Teachers were telling them to get in line. They would all be marching to the student parking lot at the front of the school until the alarm was turned off and Dardner announced everyone was to return to their classrooms.

A teacher complained loudly that there had been no announcement to staff about a fire alarm. Another teacher blamed Dardner. This was followed by the pop-pop sound of fireworks. Someone shouted for everyone to get down.

Everything went quiet.

Until the screams.

CHAPTER 3

8:28 a.m.

Amos felt the Glock pressing up against his lower back. He leaned to the side and looked out through the two narrow glass slits of the library's double door entrance at the concrete courtyard outside. A student ran by crying. The courtyard appeared to be empty.

"Attention, students and staff. This is a code blue. We are in lockdown. This is not a drill. I repeat, this is not a drill."

Amos cursed under his breath. Hearing the term code blue infuriated him. Last spring, Dardner had demanded the staff come up with a color code that would be announced should Sky Valley High face a shooting threat. The teachers immediately chose code red. Dardner was just as quick to refuse that choice. He feared red represented blood, violence, anger—all those things a school must work hard to avoid. Staff were then directed to meet for an hour after school every day until a more appropriate choice was made.

It took three weeks.

Mary Finley, the school's longtime Spanish

teacher, strongly advocated green. She felt it encompassed life, earth, and recycling. Others argued that linking green to a school shooting might confuse students and malign all the good things green was associated with. And on and on it went. From yellow, to orange, back to red, until finally a majority of staff settled on black. When that color was presented to Dardner, he was even more opposed to it than red.

"Black?" he had said. "That is totally inappropriate. Why would we ever link our students of color to such a terrible tragedy like a school shooting? That would be adding one crime onto another. Shame on you. Shame on all of us. Isn't that right, Mr. Diaz?"

Amos nearly ground the fillings out of his teeth when he heard Dardner say his name. "Keep me out of this."

Dardner's head went back as he blinked several times. "I assumed because—"

"Because what?" Amos seethed. "Because my skin is darker than yours that I would be offended by the color black or brown or fucking sepia?"

It was the first time Amos had openly cursed on the job. Dardner's pockmarked cheeks quivered as he shook his head. "No-no-no, I didn't mean anything—"

"Yeah, and that's the point. None of this means anything. For God's sake people, this is a room full of college degrees and we can't come to a consensus on a damn color? How about white? Isn't white to blame for just about everything these days? So, why not make a school shooting a code white?"

Mary Finley nodded her artificially red beehive head with great enthusiasm. "That's right," she said very seriously. "White is the true source of most of society's greatest problems. Black lives really do matter. Need I say more?" She sat back in her chair with her arms crossed while looking around the room and nodding her head, seemingly convinced she had just made the most profound statement in the history of Sky Valley High.

Amos pinched the space directly above his nose as he shook his head. "Oh my God, Mary, I was being sarcastic. I wasn't blaming white people for anything, not any more than I'd blame black or brown or purple ones."

"Purple people?" Mary said. "Are you referring to the LBGTQQ community? If so, I'd agree, we shouldn't use the color purple either. That wouldn't be fair to them."

Art Walling, the school's English teacher for the last 33 years, looked up with his jowly, basset hound-like face and scowled at Mary. "I've been using The Color Purple in my class for nearly as long as I've been teaching. Please don't tell me you're asking that I remove it from the curriculum, because, if you are, that's not going to happen. There's nothing about a school shooting in the story. It's not even applicable to this discussion. Well, except for the lesbianism."

Dardner's head snapped toward Art. "You're teaching students about lesbianism?"

"Huh?" Art said.

"I watched the movie," Mary added. "Oprah was in it. I had no idea she was a lesbian. Are you sure about that?"

It was at that point Amos had slammed both his

hands down onto the table. "Can we just a pick a damn color and go home?"

"Mr. Diaz, please," Dardner said. "We all have lives to get back to, but this is important. We're talking about school safety and that's by far the most critical aspect of our jobs—keeping kids safe. Am I right?"

A few nodded their heads. Amos wasn't among them. Dardner continued.

"Now, we've done some very good work on this issue already and I want to thank everyone for the earnest discussion. Clearly, we need to eliminate the colors black, green and purple from consideration. There appears to be some disagreement on white so for the sake of moving things along let's go ahead and put that color aside as well, so long as that's okay with all of you?"

Everyone, even Amos, nodded. Dardner smiled. "Great," he said. "I'd like to make a suggestion. I was thinking of the color blue because blue represents police and the police are who we'll be calling if we ever face a shooting scenario. It's a non-offensive color but also a logical one given its connection to law enforcement. So how about it?"

Amos cleared his throat. "I think you should have made that decision weeks ago and saved us from wasting all this time."

Dardner removed his glasses. The staff knew that was the signal he meant business. "This wasn't wasted time, Mr. Diaz. I'm sorry you don't see it that way."

"Whatever," Amos said. "Code blue it is."

"If that's what staff agrees to," Dardner replied.

Art held both his hands up in front of him. "Just so

I'm clear, nobody is trying to censor me from assigning The Color Purple to my students, right?"

Dardner put his glasses back on. "Actually, I will need to talk to you about that later, Mr. Walling."

Art's face tightened. "Ah shit," he muttered.

Dardner nodded. "Okay, it appears code blue will be the signal to all staff who we are dealing with an on-campus shooting. Of course, we all hope that never happens but anyone who watches the news, especially those in education, knows these kinds of tragedies are taking place more often than they ever have. We must be prepared."

"That's not true."

Everyone looked at Amos. Dardner arched a brow. "What's not true, Mr. Diaz?"

"There aren't more school shootings than ever before. In fact, school shootings are way down. It's media coverage of the shootings that are up."

"That's ridiculous," Dardner said. "I don't appreciate you making a mockery of our important work here."

"I'm not mocking the work. Go ahead and have a code for a school shooting scenario. I'm fine with that. You're right. It's prudent to be prepared. What I'm not fine with is your misrepresentation of reality. School shootings are down dramatically since the 1990s. An average of ten students a year die from school-related gun violence. I am not minimizing any loss of life but that's ten deaths out of 56 million students attending schools in this country. 700% more kids under the age of 14 die from drowning, yet I don't see anyone out in the streets marching against water."

Dardner bit down on his lower lip as he clenched his fists at his side. "Thank you for the input, Mr. Diaz. The staff has reached a decision. I'll send out a reminder to everyone in the morning regarding the code blue scenario.

When Amos got up to leave, Dardner ordered him to stay. After everyone else had left, he turned on Amos and jammed a finger into his chest. "Don't you ever embarrass me like that again. I'm the principal of this school. I'm your superior. Am I making myself clear?"

"So, the privileged white man is telling the colored man to remember his place, is that it?"

Dardner's mouth fell open. "No, that's not it at all. I would never—"

"Relax, I don't think you're a racist. You're just an insufferable moron running on too much insecurity and too little common sense."

"You can't talk to me like that."

"I just did. Now go ahead and send me that memo thing in the morning. Hell, I might even read it. Until then, I'm going home."

"Need I remind you that we're all on the same team here, Mr. Diaz?"

Amos turned around. "No, we're not. Oh, and one other thing."

"Yes?"

"You ever put a hand on me like that again, I'll lay you out. That's a promise."

Nearly a year had passed since Amos had made that promise. He now stood listening to Dardner repeating the code blue on the intercom over and over again.

"This is not a drill. Code blue. This is not a drill. Code blue. All staff and students are to seek safety immediately. Secure all classroom doors. I repeat this is not a—"

Screams. Dardner's voice shouting. The intercom went dead. Amos turned out the lights and locked the library door seconds before something pushed against it.

"Is anyone in there?"

"Who is it?" Amos answered while holding the Glock.

"It's Julia."

"Are you alone?"

"Yes. Now let me in!"

Amos peered out through the glass, confirmed Julia was alone, and unlocked the door. She pushed it open with both hands, quickly shut it behind her, and relocked it. Her face was pale, her eyes wide, and her entire body trembled.

"Oh my God," she said. "This is really happening. Here. At our school."

"Did you see the shooter?"

"No. Everyone was heading outside to the parking lot because of the fire alarm. I didn't have a class first period, so I hung back. I thought it was just a drill. The students all went through the courtyard into the main building, the cafeteria, and that's when I heard the first shot. Nobody seemed to know what it was at first. I sure didn't. I stood there frozen for a few seconds. Then people started screaming and that's when I realized what was going on. I ran back to my classroom, but I couldn't find my keys. I couldn't lock the door. I would have been a sitting duck. So, I came here."

"Did anyone see you?"

"I don't know. Why?"

Amos looked out at the courtyard. "If the shooter saw someone come in here, he might head this way."

Julia's eyes filled with tears. "Oh, I'm sorry. I didn't mean to put you in danger, Amos."

"Goodness no, that's not what I meant. I'm glad you came. This is as safe a place as any on campus. There's only one way in and a fire escape door at the back. You're one of the few people here I wouldn't want to see get hurt."

Julia wiped her eyes and cocked her head. "What do you mean? Why would you want anyone to get hurt?"

That is when she noticed the gun and backed away until her shoulders struck the door behind her.

"Amos, what are doing with that?"

Amos jammed the gun into the small of his back and then held up both hands to show he was no longer holding it. "It's just for protection."

"But guns aren't allowed at school. It's against the law." Julia's eyes got big. "Is that why you told me this morning I should stay in my room? Were you warning me? Do you have something to do with what's happening?"

"No, I don't. I swear. I'm just as confused by what's going on out there as you are."

Another shot came from inside the main building adjacent to the courtyard. Whoever was doing the shooting was getting closer to the library. Julia put both hands over her mouth and started to weep. Amos pulled her close. Her body stiffened as she tried to push away. He gently cupped the back of her head with his hand. After a few seconds, she relented and hugged him tight.

"I don't want to die."

"You won't die. Not today."

Julia looked up and stared into Amos's dark eyes. "Promise?"

"Yeah, I promise."

CHAPTER 4

8:49 a.m.

"Let's move to the back. It'll be safer there."
Julia nodded but kept quiet while staring at the floor. Amos took her by the hand and led her to the office.

"Did you call 911?"

Amos rolled a chair over to Julia and had her sit down. "No," he said. "Did you?"

"I tried. I couldn't get through."

"Probably because all the students and other teachers are calling in at the same time. I'm sure the authorities know. They might even be out there already. We'll be fine here. The lights are out. The doors are locked."

"Could we sneak out the fire escape door in the back?"

"Only if we absolutely have to. We open that door and the alarm goes off. They'll know someone is in here."

Julia took out her phone. "Let me see if there's anything on the news yet."

Amos watched and waited. Julia looked up.

"Nothing."

"It's early," Amos said. "People know. Help is on the way. You want a glass of water?"

"I'm fine, thanks. It seems so quiet now. No more gunshots."

"Maybe the cops took out the shooter already."

Julia's eyes begged for it to be true. "You think?"

"Could be. We have to stay positive."

"Why?"

"Positive thoughts make for positive energy. Negative thoughts make for negative energy."

"I never took you for someone who believed in that kind of thing."

"What? The power of positive thinking?"

Julia's smile warmed the space between Amos and her. "All due respect, Mr. Diaz, but you always struck me as..."

"Yeah?"

"Well, negative."

Amos shrugged. "Sure, about certain things."

"Like this job? Dardner?"

"I suppose. Don't you ever just want to scream? Hit something? Rip someone a new one?"

"Not really. Right now, I just want everyone to get home safely."

"Me too."

Julia frowned. "What is it?" Amos asked her.

"You have a gun."

"Uh-huh. We already established that."

"Shouldn't you help the people outside? Maybe you could use it to kill the shooter."

"That would mean I'd be leaving you alone in here.

Besides, it's like you said. We haven't heard any gunshots for a while. The shooter might already be dead."

Julia glanced up at the ceiling with narrowed eyes. "No, there would have been an all clear announced over the intercom or at least something to let us know help is on the way."

"Give it a little more time."

"We shouldn't just be sitting here hiding. You're armed. You could help save a lot of people."

"Or get shot."

"What happened to positive thinking?"

"I'm positive we should stay right here."

Julia pointed at the phone on the desk next to Amos. "We could call the office."

"What if the shooter is there? He'd see the caller identification and know the call came from the library."

"So? Let him come and then you shoot him."

"It wouldn't be wise to invite a confrontation, especially when there's no need to."

"I never took you for a coward."

"Good, because I'm not."

"I think you are a coward, Amos."

"You don't mean that. It's the stress talking."

"It's not the stress. It's the truth. I can't believe you're just going to hide out in here when you could be doing something to help. You leave. I'll lock the door. You and your gun go check what's going on out there. That's what you should be doing."

"But I promised to keep you safe. Did you already forget that?"

"Don't use me as your excuse for wanting to just sit here and hide instead of being out there helping."

Amos looked away.

"What?" Julia said. "Did I hurt your feelings? If I did, I have news for you. I don't care. Give me the gun. I'll go out there."

"Let's wait a little longer, okay? "

"That's wasting time. Either you do something, or I will."

Amos closed the office door. "We're staying right here. You're being irrational."

Julia stood. "Are you holding me hostage?"

"Don't be ridiculous. I'm trying to keep you safe."

"By keeping me a prisoner?"

Amos's eyes flared. "Goddammit! Sit your ass down!"

Julia dropped into the chair so hard she nearly fell over backwards. Amos grabbed her wrist and tugged her forward.

"Don't touch me."

Amos let go. "I was just trying to keep you from falling." He looked at her. She glared at him.

"Fine," he said. "I'll go outside but you have to promise to lock the door behind me and don't let anyone else in until I get back. Understood?"

"Really?"

"Yeah." Amos motioned for Julia to follow him out of the office. "C'mon."

When they reached the door, Amos put his face up to the glass and peered out at the courtyard. "Looks empty and it's still quiet." He was holding the Glock.

"Do you know how to use that?"

Amos glanced at the gun and nodded. "Sure, I think so."

"You think so?"

"Point and shoot, right?"

"Where'd you get it?"

"It was my father's."

"Have you used it before?"

"What's with all the questions? Do you want me to go out there or not?"

"It's your choice. I'm not making you do anything you don't want to do."

Amos shook his head. "You sound like my ex-wife."

"Stacy?"

"Yeah."

Amos unlocked the door, grasped the handle, and took a deep breath. "Remember," he said. "You lock this door as soon as I close it behind me and don't let anyone inside until I get back."

Julia nodded. "Got it." She put her hand on Amos's shoulder. "Please be careful."

Amos took another deep breath and whispered a countdown to himself. "Three, two, one..."

The intercom in the wall over their heads crackled to life. Julia flinched and squeaked as she looked up. Amos slammed the door lock back into place.

"This is Principal Dardner. All staff and students should be in their first period classrooms. I repeat, all staff and students should be in their first period classrooms with all entrance and exit points secured. Please remain there until further instructions are announced. All code white protocols remain in place. Do not leave your classrooms until further notice.

Thank you."

Amos and Julia looked at each other and blurted out the same question at the same time. "Code white?"

Amos shrugged. "Let's go back into the office."

"What the hell is code white?"

"I don't know but I don't like it." Amos sat down and motioned for Julia to join him.

"Did Dardner just get it wrong?" she asked.

"Not likely. If it was just a mistake, he would be back on the intercom correcting it by now."

"Then why'd he say it?"

"Maybe it was a warning. Did he sound right to you?"

Julia shook her head. "No. He actually sounded terrified."

"That's what I thought. Like a man with a gun to his head."

"So, what do we do now?"

Amos got up holding the Glock. "I go ahead and do what I was already getting ready to do—take a look outside."

Julia's eyes widened. "But Dardner said we're supposed to stay in our classrooms."

"So?"

Julia followed Amos to the exit. "Wait." She stood up on her toes and lightly kissed his cheek. "Keep your promise. Be back quick."

"That's what every inch of my cowardly body intends to do."

Amos stepped outside.

The door locked behind him.

CHAPTER 5

9:14 a.m.

Amos encountered a boy standing across the courtyard holding a gun. He wore mud-stained camo pants, a t-shirt, baseball cap, and hiking boots. They both froze when they saw each other. Amos made sure to point his weapon at the ground. The boy had a 22. rifle. He glanced down at the Glock, looked up at Amos, and then pointed the rifle at him.

"I'm not here to hurt you," Amos said. "Are you alone?"

The boy shook his head.

"Is your last name Burke?"

"How'd you know that?"

"Lucky guess. Are your dad and brother here with you?"

"None of your business."

"Are you a student at the middle school?"

"Maybe."

"Were you the one who started the fire there this morning?"

The boy regripped the rifle. "You're supposed to be in your classroom. Didn't you hear the announcement?"

"My name is Mr. Diaz. I'm a teacher here. What's your name?"

"Waylon."

"Waylon Burke?"

"I don't talk to teachers. Go back to your classroom."

"Why are you out here with a gun, Waylon?"

Waylon lifted the rifle up, so he could wipe his nose with the back of his hand. "Standing guard."

"How old are you?"

"Gonna be twelve next month."

"So, you're in the 6th grade, huh? How do you like it?"

"Like what?"

"School."

"Hate it."

"Why?"

"If you don't stop talking to me, I'm gonna shoot you."

"You'd really do that, Waylon? Is that because your dad told you to? Or your older brother Walter?"

"You know them?"

"Actually, your dad Willy was a student of mine a long time ago. Can I talk to him? Your father?"

Waylon shook his head. "You don't want that."

"Why not?"

"He'll kill you."

"And why would he do that?"

"Because he hates all of you for what you did to him and our family."

"I didn't do anything to your father, Waylon."

Waylon's eyes narrowed. "Ain't you a teacher?"

"I am."

"Then he hates you and so does my brother. Now go away."

"I'd rather stay here and talk with you some more. Can you tell me where the other students and teachers are?"

"In their classrooms where they're supposed to be. Where you should be."

"Is anyone hurt?"

Waylon's head turned toward the sound of a door opening. "Hey, asshat, who are you talking to?"

Waylon pointed to where Amos had been standing but Amos was no longer there. "It was a teacher. He had a gun and kept asking me questions."

Amos peaked around the corner and saw an older, taller, and leaner version of Waylon standing in the courtyard. He was dressed similarly and holding an assault rifle. "What the hell are you talking about?" the older boy said. "I don't see nobody."

"Yeah, he was right over there. Said his name was Mr. Diaz. You know him?"

"Heard of him. Where'd he go?"

Waylon shrugged. "Don't know. Walter, I promise. He was right over there. You want me to try and find him?"

"Nah, you stay put. I'll check it out."

Walter's footsteps echoed against the concrete walls. "Shit," Amos whispered as he quickly hid behind a vending machine in a corridor adjacent to the courtyard. He pressed his back against the wall, sucked in his stomach, held his breath, and waited.

"Was he over here?" Walter yelled to his little brother.

"Yeah, he was standing right there."

Amos gripped the Glock tighter as Walter entered the corridor. "You in here, teacher? Better hope not because my family don't play. I'll fuck you up for real."

Sirens wailed in the distance. A phone rang. Walter answered it.

"Hey. Yeah, I hear them. I'm outside. Waylon said he saw a teacher with a gun in the courtyard. That's right—a gun. Not sure. I don't see anything. Maybe he's freaking out, seeing things. He is just a kid. Okay. Fine. I said okay. We'll be right there."

Walter put his phone away and turned around. "You hear those sirens, right? This is all about to get real now, Waylon. Dad wants to see us in the principal's office. Let's go."

"What about the teacher?"

"Hell if I know. There's nobody here."

"You sure?"

"If someone else was here, they're gone now."

"But he had a gun."

"Did he? If he had a gun, why didn't he try and shoot you with it?"

"Because he's just a stupid teacher. Probably don't know how."

"Exactly. Why would a teacher have a gun? Teachers don't fight. They cry and complain and take summers off. If he was here, he was probably carrying a book or a ruler or something, and even if it was a gun, I bet he don't know how to use it. Either way, we have more important things to worry about. There's a shit-ton of cops filling up the parking lot outside. Let's go hear what Dad has to say. We shouldn't keep him waiting."

Walter returned to the courtyard, waited for Waylon to join him, and then they left together. Amos could feel his heart pounding madly in his chest and looked down to see his hands trembling. His knees buckled as the Glock nearly dropped from his hand.

"Jesus, pull yourself together."

He walked out from behind the vending machine, crept down the corridor, looked out into the courtyard, and found it empty. The entrance doors into the main building were closed. Sunlight bathed the courtyard concrete, warming it under Amos's feet. He looked to the right, to the left, and then jogged to the library. The door was locked. He knocked twice and waited. Julia looked up at him from behind the glass slit and opened the door. Amos nearly fell as he crossed the door's threshold.

"Hurry, shut it," he gasped.

Julia locked the door. "What happened out there? Did you see anyone else?"

Amos shuffled to the back of the library, went into the office, put the gun on the desk, and sat down. He bent forward until his head was nearly between his knees. Julia touched his shoulder.

"Are you okay? Can I get you something?"

Amos sat up. When Julia saw his face, her eyes widened. "You don't look so good. Can I get you some water?"

"I think I might be having a heart attack."

"What?"

"Yeah, my heart is hammering. It won't slow down. I can't catch my breath."

Julia's eyes darted around the office as she bit down on her lip. "Oh no. Uh, does you left arm hurt? Your shoulder?"

"Maybe. I'm not sure. I just need to breathe."

"Wait. How about aspirin? Yeah, that's supposed to help for a heart attack. Or is it a stroke? Shit. I don't know."

"Aspirin might help. You know where to get some?"

"Yeah, open the desk drawer right in front of you. Ronda always keeps some handy."

Amos opened the drawer and found the aspirin. He also found something else and set both items on the top of the desk. Julia smiled.

"Oh! You found her other little helper."

It was a nearly full bottle of Smirnoff. Amos put three aspirin tablets in his palm and washed them down with the vodka. He grimaced, held the bottle out in front of him, and then took another swig.

"That's better," he said while taking in several slow, deep breaths.

Julia's brows arched. "Yeah? You sure?"

Amos nodded. "Much better. I think it was just a panic attack."

Julia sat down. "Over what?"

"I saw a kid in the courtyard with a gun. Then his brother showed up. He had a gun too. A big one. I thought I might have to shoot them."

"Why didn't you?"

"What? Shoot two kids?"

Julia folded her arms across her chest. "Are you kidding? When you see two armed students running around the school, you take them out before anyone else gets hurt."

"When I woke up this morning, I would have agreed with you, but actually having a weapon in your hand while you're looking at another human being, it's more complicated than that. I'm not someone who can just start shooting people down. And you know what? I'm okay with that."

Julia glanced at the Glock and then looked at Amos. "If you can't do it, I will."

Amos pulled the gun toward him. "I didn't say I can't do it. I chose not to because I didn't have to. As far as we know, nobody's been hurt yet. I said I'd keep you safe. If someone comes through those doors out there intending to do us harm, I'll do what needs to be done, but until then, we wait."

"Those who can, do; those who can't, teach."

"What's that supposed to mean?"

Julia drank from the bottle of vodka then pushed it toward Amos. "It means I'm hoping when the time comes for action around here, you're a doer and not a teacher. I'm so scared right now. More scared than I've ever been in my entire life. It's all I can do to sit here and keep it together. I don't want to die. What I do want is to walk out of this place on my own two feet, not carried out in a body bag. You have a gun. You better be ready and willing to use it. If that means blowing one of those little shits out there to kingdom come, then so be it. I need a doer right now, a man, not a teacher. Are you hearing me, Mr. Diaz?"

Amos took a long drink from the bottle, set it down, and leveled his gaze onto Julia. "Loud and clear, Ms. Hodson."

CHAPTER 6

9:27 a.m.

When Amos's phone started ringing, he nearly dropped it. He glanced at Julia. "It's a district number," he said.

"Hurry—answer it."

Amos put the phone to his ear. "Hello?"

"Mr. Diaz?"

"Yes."

"Is it safe for you to talk?"

"Yes."

"Good. This is Officer Markley. We spoke earlier today in the library. Is that where you are now?"

"It is."

"Are you alone?"

Amos shook his head as he answered. "No. I'm here with Julia Hodson."

"The art teacher?"

"That's correct."

There was a long pause. Amos glanced at the phone thinking the connection was lost.

"Mr. Diaz?"

"Yes, I'm still here."

"How much of the situation are you aware of?"

"I heard gunfire. Dardner instructed staff and students to remain in their rooms. I also saw two armed students in the courtyard just a little while ago."

"Did they see you?"

"One of them, yes, but they don't know where I'm at now."

There was another long pause.

"Do you know the names of the armed students?"

"Walter and Waylon Burke. They mentioned their father is in the main office."

"This is all very good information, Mr. Diaz. Thank you. Are you aware of any injuries or fatalities to students or staff?"

"No. Are you calling me from the parking lot?"

"Yes. There's a significant law enforcement presence gathering outside the school."

"I would imagine there is. What's the plan? Have you been in contact with Principal Dardner or Mr. Burke?"

"I'm sorry, Mr. Diaz, but I'm not allowed to answer that right now."

The intercom turned on. "Wait," Amos said. "Something's happening."

It was Dardner. He sounded tired, like a rubber band being stretched to its limit.

"Staff and students of Sky Valley High, please listen carefully. You are to now leave your classrooms and walk as quietly and orderly as possible into the courtyard. There is to be no talking. Do not attempt to enter the main office. Do not attempt to escape. All the primary exits have already been secured. Those currently in the parking lot at the front of the school, including law enforcement, are not to approach the building. There are to be no helicopters flying overhead. Failure to follow these instructions will lead to serious consequences for everyone involved. Thank you."

"What's going on?" Markley asked.

Amos went to the door and looked out. "You heard the announcement, right?"

"Yeah."

"Well, that's what's happening. The courtyard is filling up with staff and students."

"Does anyone appear injured?"

"No. The students look more confused than scared. Most of them are texting on their phones."

"Yeah, we have their parents out here doing the same. How many do you think are in the courtyard?"

"A couple hundred at most. Where are the rest?"

Amos could hear Markley reporting the number to someone else. "A lot of them got out right after the shots were fired," he said. "Some of the staff indicated they knew something was up when Dardner announced a code white because there is no code white, so they took their classes out of the main building using the secondary exits. They're all standing behind the barricades we have set up out here. The media are showing up in droves now too. This is shaping up to be one hell of a Monday."

"Indeed, it is. Who were you talking to?"

"County sheriff. They're heading the law enforcement response as of right now. State patrol and the feds are on their way as well. I'm the acting liaison between the district and the county."

"How'd you know to call me?"

"Educated hunch. You weren't among the staff who got out earlier."

"Have you been in contact with Dardner?"

"No. I tried. He's not picking up. At least after hearing the announcement, we now know he's okay."

"Should we join the others in the courtyard?"

Again, there was a long pause before Markley replied. "No. We prefer you and Ms. Hodson to remain in the library. It'll be safest for you there, and you can hopefully provide us updates on what's going on inside the school. Are you willing to do that, Mr. Diaz?"

"Of course. Whatever it takes to help get everyone home safe."

"Keep your phone close. I'll check back in soon. Don't contact anyone else and let me know if the situation in the courtyard changes. Oh, and stay out of sight."

The call ended. "That was Officer Markley," Amos said.

Julia put her face up to the door and looked out at the courtyard. "So, when are they coming to get us out of here?"

"Not sure. He didn't tell me much."

"Why do you think that is?"

Amos shrugged. "I don't know."

Julia stepped back from the door. "Maybe he doesn't trust you."

"What do you mean?"

"If the shooters get a hold of us, Markley doesn't want you telling them what they know. Or, he realizes you're hiding something from him. Maybe it's both."

"I didn't hide anything from him. Why would I do that?"

"The hell you didn't. Did you forget you were holding it in your other hand while you were talking to him?"

Amos slid the Glock into the back of his pants. "Is there something you'd like to say to me?"

"Okay, fine. I'm wondering why you didn't mention to Markley anything about the gun. Why the secrets, Amos? What are you hiding? Are you actually working with the shooters?"

"What?"

"You heard me. Sure, it sounds crazy, but is it any crazier than you showing up to work with a weapon on the same day all this other shit goes down? That's one hell of a coincidence." Julia took out her phone. "I'm calling the district office. I want answers—real answers. Not the crap you've been feeding me."

"No!" Amos snatched the phone away.

"What the hell do you think you're doing? Give it back. Now."

"Markley said we weren't to contact anyone else other than him."

Julia's lips drew back as she spit the words out between tightly clenched teeth. "That's bullshit. Give me my phone."

"I won't do that. Go sit down."

"Or what? You going to shoot me?"

"Stop acting like a child."

"I will as soon as you stop acting like such a dick."

Amos shook his head and sighed. "Fucking teachers."

"You want to explain that comment? Last I checked you are a fucking teacher."

"Just be quiet."

"Give me back my phone and I will."

Amos dropped the phone on the floor, paused, then smashed it under the heel of his shoe until nothing was left but fragments. His breath hissed through his nostrils.

"Go back in the office, sit down, and shut up you self-important little bitch."

Julia flicked a tear away from her cheek. "You're crazy. I'll take my chances out there rather than be stuck in here with you."

Amos blocked the door. "For Christ's sake, stop and think. You go out there and people could die. Do you understand? Do you even care? I'm sorry for calling you a bitch, okay? I mean that. I shouldn't have said it."

"You broke my phone."

"And I apologize for that as well. Here, you don't believe me when I say Markley told me not to communicate with anyone else? Use my phone. Call him back and ask him. He'll tell you."

Amos held his phone out as Julia stared at it. "Go ahead," he said.

Julia's shoulders slumped. Her eyes closed. "Maybe I was being a bit of a bitch."

"Yeah, you were."

When Julia looked up, Amos was smiling back at

her. "You really are a dick," she said.

"I won't argue that."

Amos put his arm around Julia's shoulders. Her body tightened at first, but then she relaxed and walked with him to the back office. After they sat down, they heard a chopper pass over the school.

"Those things better not get too close," Amos said. "Dardner's instructions said no helicopters."

"Why do you think the shooters have everyone lined up in the courtyard?"

"I don't know."

"Are they going to kill them?"

Amos gave the same answer. "I don't know."

"If you hear gunshots, will you run out there and try and save them?"

"Absolutely."

Julia looked like she didn't believe him.

Amos looked like he didn't care.

CHAPTER 7

9:57 a.m.

"I have to use the bathroom."

Amos shook his head. "That's not a good idea."

"I didn't say anything about a good idea. I said I have to use the bathroom."

"You could just pee in the sink. I won't look."

Julia shifted in her chair. "First, that's disgusting. Second, I don't have to go pee."

"Oh."

"Yeah, and it's feeling like something I'm going to need to take care of pretty quick. I'm really starting to percolate over here."

"No way you can hold on until the feeling passes?"

Julia's face tightened. "I don't think so. That morning coffee is kicking in big time. I have a touch of IBS. The coffee, all the stress...this could get messy. I really need to get to a bathroom."

Amos tapped his fingers on the table. "Okay, let's go have a look."

The courtyard remained full of staff and students. Most of the cell phones had been put away, replaced by faces that were finally showing the strain of what was happening to them. It wasn't a game or a social media video they could watch and then turn off. This was real. They were in danger—and they all knew it.

Amos pointed at something. "That's the kid with the rifle I saw earlier, Waylon Burke. He's in the same spot on the other side of the courtyard. I don't see his brother, but we have to assume he's close."

Julia's eyes darted from side to side as she peered through the glass. "The bathroom is right across the hall. I'll sneak over without anyone seeing me."

"You better hope it's that simple."

Julia put a hand on her stomach and groaned. "I really don't have much choice. Let me out. Hurry."

"We don't want anyone knowing we're in here. Don't stop. Don't signal to someone. Just use the bathroom and get right back here, okay?"

"Yes, sir."

Amos unlocked the door and cracked it open just enough to allow Julia to crawl through on her hands and knees across the dirty concrete. When she reached the bathroom entrance, she sat with her back against the wall and looked at Amos. He scanned the courtyard for any sign of trouble and then nodded to her. She grabbed hold of the door handle, pulled it open, and disappeared inside.

A minute went by.

Then another.

And then another.

After five minutes, Amos took out the Glock and prepared to check on Julia. He gripped and regripped the door handle, looked outside, looked away, and then repeated the process. "Goddammit," he whispered.

Amos opened the door.

The intercom came on.

He closed the door and looked up.

"This is Principal Dardner. I know law enforcement personnel can hear me in the parking lot. I urge them to remain outside the building. Do not attempt to enter. If that happens, people will be hurt. I repeat, people will be hurt. As of right now, there have been no injuries. No one has been shot. We are all well."

There was a scuffling sound and then a deeper voice saying something in the background. Dardner cleared his throat.

"Uh, very soon, you will hear from the man responsible for what is happening here today. His name is William—"

The intercom shut off. Amos stood with his mouth hanging half-open and waited. Ten seconds went by before the intercom came back on.

"His name is Willy Burke. He's a former student of Sky Valley High, and he is here today visiting with his sons, Walter and Waylon. Walter is of course a valued student at the high school while Waylon attends the middle school just down the road from us. Mr. Burke, are you ready?"

The deeper voice was heard more clearly. "Yeah, I'm ready."

Another long pause. More shuffling. Breathing.

"I'm Willy Burke. This place kicked me out once. Now it's trying to do the same to my boy Walter. That ain't right. None of it. You people, people like the principal standing next to me, you're all going to listen to what I have to say. All you cops in the parking lot? Same thing. Fucking listen for once, okay? You might think I'm some loser freak, but I'm not. I'm like a whole lot of other people in this world who nobody wants to hear from. Well, you're gonna hear me now because I'm gonna speak for all of us. Words, I'm not so good with them, but today, I'll do my best. Just shut up and listen. That's all I ask. Then this can be over. People can go home. You students in the courtyard, I want you to take out all those fancy phones and send this message to the world. We can't trust the cops or these teachers or this principal to speak the truth. At least not my truth, not your truth, not our truth. The only truth they know is their own, and that truth is shit. It's a lie, and I've had enough of it, and I'm sure some of you have had enough of it too.

"The thing is, the government used to pay me to kill people. Didn't pay much but the checks always cashed, so I didn't complain. Did a tour in Afghanistan and another couple in Iraq. Just a high school dropout slinging an M16 for Uncle Sam. Spent most my time over there trying not to die. Kill or be killed I guess. Plenty of others around me did the same. It's not anything like the movies or television. War isn't cool. It's not exciting or brave or heroic. It just sucks.

"So, I did my service and then I came back home. I came here. And what do I get for all that time I spent over there risking my life for reasons I still don't understand? I tell you what me and a few other fellas got—a fucking parade. That's just another way of saying I got shit. Sure as hell wasn't what I needed. Six months back and the bank was moving to foreclose our house and my wife, well, she didn't stick around to see how long it'd take them to do it. I hate her for that, but I don't blame her. Guess a parade wasn't good enough for her either. What I needed was a job, but nobody would take a chance on a high school dropout ex-soldier. Seems I wasn't good enough or smart enough. I went off to war for a man called Bush. I came home to another one called Obama. Both them bastards promised I'd be taken care of and they both lied. Maybe this other fella will be better. Maybe not. I'm not holding my breath. Republican? Democrat? Don't nobody talk to me about that shit. I don't have time for stupid titles only meant to keep us all divided and fighting each other.

"Lost the house. No job. Lots of bills. Kids who needed to be taken care of. What's a man to do? Life can be a very dark place, you know? I've been choking on that darkness for a long time now. Only thing kept me going was the hope it would be better for my boys. That they'd have the chances I wasn't given. I looked people in the eye and tried to smile. Not too many of you ever bothered to smile back.

"Wasn't a job I was too proud to take. All my boys have ever known are hand-me-downs. But they say school is where things can equal out. That's what the teachers and the principals and the counselors and all of them other so-called experts say. That it don't matter where you come from because an education can be your ticket out.

"Bullshit. More fucking lies. This school has been hassling my Walter since he got here. And for what?

Being the son of a dropout? A kid with the wrong last name? I'm not saying my boys are perfect. Hell no. Not even close. They run me ragged. But they're not the devils this place would make them out to be. Walter's been fighting for a chance here. Every damn day, he's been fighting. You hit him, he hits back. That's what he was taught to do. You want to blame someone for that, then go on and blame me. I put that in him to do what he done. People say we sell drugs. That's a lie. People say we steal. That's a lie. People say we cheat. Lies and more lies. I've had my fill. No more. Now it's our turn.

"My boys have gone hungry, but they never starved. I've always provided as best I could, but I've about broke my body doing it, and I worry my spirit isn't far behind. Now here we are: me, my boys, and all of you. I didn't come here to hurt nobody. I know I said some things that spoke of doing something different yesterday, but that was just my temper talking. That isn't to say I can't hurt someone. Lord knows I've hurt plenty. It's just, well, I can't allow what was done to me to be done to my boys. They don't deserve it. They come here dressed in the same clothes they wore the day before, the week before, the month before because it's all they got to wear. And for that, they're forced to put up with the looks, the whispers, the cruel jokes and sometimes, they smack a mouth for it. Big fucking deal. Those kids have it coming. They need to learn that a smart mouth can lead to a busted one. That's how the world used to be, and it was a whole lot better than this thing we call a world now.

"Last year, I helped a man with a flat tire. He was about my age. Drove a real nice car. Saw him standing on the side of the road holding a jack in one hand and a lug wrench in the other. He had no idea what to do with those things. This fella couldn't change a goddamn tire to save his life. So, I walked over and did it for him. That's when I find out he's a teacher here at the high school, and I can't help but think, how in the hell does a man like him—he's less than a man who can't even change a tire - how is it he's someone with so much power over the future of so many kids like my boys?"

Willy wasn't quite shouting into the intercom, but he was close.

"I mean, c'mon! A grown-ass man can't change a tire on his Lexus? As I'm tightening up the last of the lug nuts, I couldn't help but wonder who was wiping his ass for him. What's going on in these schools? Where did the shop classes go? I learned how to tear a motor down in this same high school when I was a freshman, and all these years later, there's a man teaching kids here who can't change his own tire. I don't care who you are or how you want to spin it, we all know down deep that's fucked up.

"And these are the same people who think they can kick my kid out for standing up for himself? For his little brother? No. No way. You can all go to hell if you think I'm gonna take that sitting down. Today, you put the soy milk and lattes down. Today, you get a taste of real American red meat. Today is a different kind of lesson and you will fucking learn something or I'm gonna die trying to teach it to you. That's no joke.

I'm ready. Are you?"

The intercom shut off. Amos continued staring at it.

"What the hell was that?" he said to himself. He heard a noise, turned around, cocked his head, and waited to hear it again.

"Amos."

It was Julia whispering his name as she stood on the other side of the door with her face pressed against the glass. "Hurry. Open up before someone sees me."

Amos reached down to pull the door open and then his hand drew back. His eyes narrowed as he took a few seconds to confirm what he thought he saw.

Julia wasn't alone.

CHAPTER 8

10:16 a.m.

"What's he doing here?" Amos hissed. "I found him hiding in the other stall in the bathroom," Julia answered. "I'm sure he was nearly as embarrassed as I was. The noises coming out of me, let me tell you, it wasn't pretty. He's scared like everyone else. I couldn't just leave him there."

Amos shook his head. "He's trouble."

"Trouble? He's a student. You would have rather I left him in the bathroom? That's crazy."

"He could get us all killed."

Randal Risen was still wearing the same puffy black jacket he had on earlier that morning. He watched Amos and Julia talking about him from a chair on the other side of the library.

"It's done," Julia said. "He's here. Get over it."

Amos turned around and stared at Randal. "Why aren't you in the courtyard with all the others?"

Randal adjusted the wide brim baseball cap on his head. "Same reason you're not, right? People out there with guns and shit."

"I take it you weren't in your first period class like

you were supposed to be. Still cruising the hallways looking for more young girls to harass?"

Randal folded his arms over his chest and tilted his head back. "Fuck you."

Amos strode across the library with the Glock pointed at Randal's face. "No, fuck you."

"What the hell, Amos?" Julia struggled to pull Amos's arm down. "Put that away."

"Hey," Randal said. "Why do you have a gun? This is a gun-free zone. You're a teacher. Isn't that, like, illegal or something?"

Amos pressed the tip of the Glock into the center of Randal's forehead. "Shut up, you little shit."

"Stop it!" Julia shouted. "Have you lost your mind? He's just a kid."

"He's no kid. He's a plague. Him and everyone like him."

Randal appeared ready to cry. "I'm sorry, man."

"Sorry for what?" Amos said.

Randal blinked several times. "Uh, for telling you to fuck off?"

Amos kept the gun pointed at Randal's head. "Well, look at you. Getting respectable-like all of sudden."

Julia stepped in front of Amos and pushed him back. "That's enough. You're scaring him."

"You mind getting your disgusting ass out of my face? Your digestion is seriously messed up. I heard it. Smelled it too."

Julia's head snapped around as she looked down at Randal. "Excuse me?"

"I'm just saying that after what came out of you in

the bathroom, I don't want your shitter in my face, okay?"

"Mr. Diaz is right. You are a little asshole."

"Whatever lady. Just keep yours away from me."

Amos stepped around Julia and cracked the side of Randal's skull with the butt of his gun. "I told you to shut up."

Randal dropped out of the chair. Blood trickled down his cheek. He turned over, dabbed the blood with the tips of his fingers and then stared at it wide-eyed.

"You hit me," he whispered. "You really hit me."

"Feel fortunate that's all I did to you and your filthy mouth."

Randal pushed himself up off the floor and stood glaring at Amos. "I'm gonna get you fired." He held his bloody fingers in front of Amos's face. "For this. You're done. I'm suing your ass."

He pointed at Julia. "And if you don't back me, I'll sue you too. You'll lose your job just like him."

"Wait," Julia said. "Let's all just calm down. The only thing that matters is all of us getting out of here alive. The real enemies are the ones holding the staff and students hostage in the courtyard, right?"

Randal shook his head. "He's going down. You saw. Teachers can't hit kids. Not ever. And he did it with a fucking gun."

"Ms. Hodson didn't see anything," Amos said. "You fell. That's how you hurt your head."

When Amos tried to look at Julia for confirmation, she avoided his eyes. Randal grinned. "See? She knows what time it is. Yeah, she knows I'm right."

Amos grabbed hold of Julia's arm and walked her toward the back office. "He fell, right? That's what you saw."

Julia jerked her arm free. "What about the gun, Amos? You can't expect me to lie about everything for you. I'm sorry. I have my own career to consider here."

"Your career? You're a goddamn art teacher."

"That's right, I am, and I happen to care about this place and most of the people in it."

"Pathetic. You'd choose to protect that piece of shit instead of me?"

"It's not about protecting anyone. It's the truth. You hit Randal. That's what happened. I can't unsee it. I'm sorry."

"Yeah, so am I. You know, I've been at this a lot longer than you. I can remember when teachers felt like we were in this thing together. There was an unspoken understanding that we supported one another. These days? Shit. You all go around using words like supportive, collaborative, and consensus, but it's a lie. It's really all about covering your own ass, and that's a big reason why these schools are such a mess. Everybody's running scared and nobody has the balls to fix it."

"I don't care about the old days, Amos. There's nothing right about a teacher striking a student. It's like climate change and social justice. Some things are non-negotiable truths."

Amos wiped his hand over his face as he shook his head. "I had no idea you were so naïve. Thanks for clearing it up. At least now when I look at you, I know exactly what I'm looking at."

"Right back at you, Mr. Diaz."

"Fine. When we get out of here, the little shit presses charges, sues me, whatever. I'm tired of thinking the world could be different. It is what it is."

"You did it to yourself. You shouldn't have hit him."

Amos smiled. "No, you're right. What I should have done was put this gun to his head and pulled the trigger. If I'm going down, I might as well go down all the way, right?"

Julia stepped back. "What?"

"Just kidding."

"That wasn't funny, Amos. You're scaring me."

"Am I?"

"Yes. I don't like it."

"Well, then I do apologize, Ms. Hodson. Please forgive me for speaking my mind."

"I thought you were kidding."

"Sure," Amos said while nodding. "I was."

"I'd like to sit with Randal and make sure he's okay."

"Oh, by all means. He's a fine, upstanding young man. Go sit right next to him. Get close and chummy. If anyone deserves to feel safe, it's that one."

Julia brushed past Amos, walked over to Randal, and sat down next to him. "How are you two doing over there?" Amos said. "Can I get you anything?"

"Fuck you," Randal replied.

The intercom turned on. Amos, Julia, and Randal all looked up at the same time and waited.

"This is Willy Burke again. Sorry for the delay. The

cops can't seem to give me any rest with all their phone calls. Anyways, I wanted to let the people standing in the courtyard know there's a way for you all to go home. That's the honest truth. Give us what we want, and you walk out the front door. Simple as that."

There was a long pause before Willy continued. "The thing we want is Randal Risen. He's a student here, a senior, same as my boy Walter. Those two grew up together, Randal and Walter. I always considered them to be friends. Randal proved me wrong. I don't like to be wrong when it comes to knowing people. You hear me, Randal? I know you're hiding somewhere in the school. We checked the courtyard and you're not there. Now we'll start checking rooms and bathrooms until we find you. Then we're gonna make you tell everyone what you did, how you lied, and how you betrayed Walter. It's time you finally manned up, boy, and did the right thing. Don't make all these other people suffer for your mistake. And to everyone else listening right now, you can just tell us where he is, and for saving us the trouble of having to find him ourselves, we'll let you all go. I give you my word. You have ten minutes."

Julia stood up and looked down at Randal. "What is he talking about? What did you do? Is this all your fault?"

"I didn't do shit. He's crazy. The whole family is crazy."

Julia took a step back and then glanced at Amos.

"He's lying," Amos said. "Look at him. For the first time since you brought him here, he's truly afraid.

That's why he was hiding in the bathroom. He worried they'd see him trying to get out of the school. He's the one they want."

"So, what do we do?" Julia asked.

Randal got up. "What do you mean, what do you do? You keep me away from those killers out there." When Julia moved closer to Amos, Randal rolled his eyes. "Oh, I get it. Now you side with him all of a sudden because you think I'm your ticket out of here? What a cunt."

The speed Amos displayed as he closed the gap between himself and Randal stunned Julia. She stood frozen and wide-eyed watching Amos grab hold of Randal with one hand as he jammed the Glock into his mouth with the other. Randal's head rocked back. He fought to get free, but Amos held on tight and walked him backwards with the gun barrel pushed up against the back of his throat until Randal collapsed.

Amos's lips drew back as he shoved the Glock even further into Randal's mouth. Randal gasped for breath as his fingers dug into Amos's arms.

The intercom came on.

Amos looked up.

"Five more minutes. Bring Randal Risen to us and everyone in the courtyard walks out of here."

Tears streamed down Randal's cheeks. Amos took the gun out of his mouth.

"Please," Randal said. "They'll kill me. I mean it. Waylon's dad is crazy. He wants me dead."

Amos stood. When Randal tried to do the same, Amos pushed down against his chest with his foot and pointed the Glock at his face.

"Who said you could get up?"

Snot dripped over Randal's upper lip. He licked it away and then spit out a white fragment into his hand. "You broke a tooth," he said.

Amos ground his heel further into Randal's chest and grinned. "No, I didn't. You fell. Remember?"

Julia stood next to Amos. Randal looked at her. She nodded.

"That's right. You fell. That's what I saw."

Randal wiped more snot away. "You're not going to give me up to the Burkes, are you?"

Amos's grin fell like a curtain being pulled down over a dark window. His eyes went cold. He tilted his head slightly and arched a brow while staring at the whimpering, puffy-jacket-wearing lump of fear under his shoe.

"I'm not sure," he said. "I still have a few minutes to decide."

CHAPTER 9

10:34 a.m.

"Talk to me, Mr. Diaz. What the hell is going on in there?"

Amos kept the phone to his ear as he walked toward the door and looked into the courtyard. "Same as before, Officer Markley. They're all standing outside. I take it you heard the last message from Mr. Burke?"

"We sure did, and it's got us all shaking our heads out here. I know a little something about Randal Risen. He's been in trouble a time or ten. I don't suppose you know where he is?"

Randal was sitting in a chair at the back of the library near the office. Amos glanced at him and then lowered his voice. "He's not outside in the parking lot?"

"Mr. Diaz, if that was the case, why would I have asked you where he was?"

"Right. Sorry."

"So, you haven't seen him?"

"I've seen him around, sure." Amos ducked as a shadow flittered past the window. He locked eyes with Julia and put a finger to his lips and then mouthed the words get down. Julia crouched behind a bookshelf.

"What's going on?" Randal said loudly. Julia whispered to him to be quiet.

"Mr. Diaz? Are you still there?"

Amos switched the phone to his other ear. "Yeah. I think one of the Burkes just walked past the library entrance."

"Mr. Burke did say he was going to start checking rooms for Randal Risen."

"That's what I'm afraid of. You have any idea what he plans to do with Randal if he finds him?"

"No, but if that kid is still inside the school, he's got to be shitting his drawers by now. Mr. Burke put quite a bounty on his head."

"Is the cavalry about to storm the gates?"

"Can't tell you that, Mr. Diaz. What I will say is this. All of us here would sure like to see everyone walk safely out of there today."

"Are you suggesting we try and locate Randal Risen and give him over to the Burkes?"

"No, no, that's most certainly not what I'm suggesting. Let's just say the proposal has some very experienced members of law enforcement wondering what the hell Mr. Burke is up to."

"How long until they no longer feel like waiting to find out?"

"I don't know. I'm low man on the totem pole out here. The feds just arrived. It's their show now."

"Is that who's been speaking with Mr. Burke on the phone?"

"Again, I can't tell you that. I'm sorry."

"Why the hell are you bothering to call me if you can't tell me anything?"

"Because you're our eyes and ears in there, Mr. Diaz. As long as everyone in that courtyard remains safe, this situation most likely won't go from tense to shitstorm. Can you confirm if the Burkes are checking the rooms for the Risen boy yet?"

Amos peeked outside and then ducked down. "Still looks the same. The courtyard is full of people and no sign of the Burkes."

The intercom crackled to life. "Time's up," Willy Burke said. "I really wish someone would have played smart and brought Randal to me. Now, well, some of you in the courtyard will have to pay for Randal's sins. Before that happens, though, I want to tell you all about the real Randal Risen and how he's a little fucking rapist piece of shit who doesn't deserve anyone protecting him from the justice that's my right to deliver to him."

All the color left Randal's face. His head retreated into his shoulders turtle-like as he wrapped his arms around himself.

Willy continued.

"There was a little boy Randal would babysit from time to time. This was a few years ago. The family of the boy trusted Randal and welcomed him into their home. Randal abused that trust, just like he abuses most everything else he touches, including the boy. You people get my drift? You understand the monster that Randal Risen truly is and why he must pay for what he has done? My oldest son Walter tried to take care of it himself, but the school stuck their nose into it and suspended him for it. Took Randal's side. They rewarded him and punished Walter. That's when I learned about Randal's secret. Walter told me. And that's when I knew I had to do something. Not just to Randal, though. I promise he's gonna get what's coming, but so is this entire fucking school and the people who run it. The blood of today is on your hands. You won't ever forget that. I won't let you.

"I tell you what. Let's start at the top. Principal Dardner is standing next to me. How about we march him out to the courtyard right now and I put my fist through his face to prove I really do mean business. Yeah, that sounds like a good plan. Let's go."

"Can you see the courtyard, Mr. Diaz? Is Burke out there?" Markley's shouting made Amos wince as he pulled the phone away. He got up and looked out the window.

"No, not yet. Some of the students are crying. Wait. I think I see him."

Willy Burke was tall and lean, with a long and narrow, wolf-like face covered in a thick salt and pepper beard. His head was shaved. The green and tattered military jacket he wore hung off wide but bony shoulders. The sleeves were rolled up, revealing sinewy forearms covered in tattoos. The fronts of his faded blue jeans were oil-soaked, and the toes of his dirty boots marred by deep gouges. His stride was long and confident as he carried a pistol in one hand and the back of Principal Dardner's neck in the other.

"He's marching Dardner outside," Amos whispered into the phone. "And he has a gun."

"Jesus," Markley muttered. "Let's pray he doesn't do something stupid. There's a small army out here armed to the teeth. They hear gunfire and it'll be on. People will get hurt."

"Stand right there, asshole," Burke said to Dardner as he glared at the staff and students who huddled in front of him.

"Please," Dardner whimpered. "Don't hurt anyone."

Burke ran a hand across his shaved scalp. "I'm not gonna hurt anyone just yet—except you." He pointed his gun at the crowd of people. "Where's those phones you all love so much? Well, go on. Get them out. Remember what I said. We can't trust this school, the cops, the media, none of them to tell the truth. So, you record the things that happen here. Record what I have to say. Record this."

Burke's punch was hard and fast.

"Oh shit," Amos mumbled.

"What?" Markley replied. "What's going on?"

"Burke just dropped Dardner like a wet sack of grain."

"Huh?"

"He knocked the shit out of him. One punch and down he went."

Dardner was on all fours. Blood dripped from his nose and splattered onto the courtyard concrete. Burke reached down, grabbed hold of Dardner's collar, and pulled him up.

"There," Burke said. "Now everyone knows I'm a man of my word. He's okay. Just a smack to the face. If a man his age hasn't tasted his own blood by now, he's no man at all."

Markley sounded close to all-out panic. "Dammit, Diaz, what's happening?"

"Dardner's on his feet. Burke ordered the students to film it with their phones."

Amos waited. Markley didn't respond.

"Hello? You still there?"

"Yeah. We found a live stream on social media. We're looking at Burke and Dardner now. I can also see the library door in the background."

Amos heard shuffling behind him and turned around. Randal was showing Julia something on his phone. "We can see it," Julia said. Amos nodded.

"What the hell is the crazy bastard up to?" Markley asked. "And where is the Risen kid?"

Randal looked excited by the images on his phone while Julia appeared horrified.

"I need to go, Officer Markley. I have an idea."

"An idea? What are you talking about?"

Amos ended the call and turned around. "Mr. Risen."

Randal continued to stare at his phone. Amos moved toward him. "Mr. Risen, I need your attention."

Julia looked up. "What is it?"

"Mr. Risen!"

Randal rolled his eyes. "Jesus, stop with the teacher act. We're not in class. I'm busy here."

"You said you were friends with Walter Burke."

"Yeah? So?"

Amos pointed at Randal's phone. "You have his number?"

"Sure. Why?"

"Give it to me."

Randal's face scrunched up like he hadn't had a bowel movement in three days. "Why do you want Walter's number? You gonna give me up? Because if you are, then fuck you. I'm not telling you shit."

Amos took out the Glock. "You're a slow learner."

Julia got up and moved to the side.

"Wait," Randal said. "Put the goddamn gun away. Fine, I'll give you his number."

"Pull it up," Amos said.

Randal's hands shook as he scrolled through his contact list. "There—got it."

"Give it here."

"Can't I just tell you the number? C'mon man, I don't want to lose my phone."

"Mr. Risen, if you don't hand over your phone now, I'm going to return this gun to the back of your throat. Is that what you want?"

"Tell me why you want Walter's number."

Amos held his hand out. "I don't have to tell you anything. Your phone. Now."

"You better hope I never take that gun from you, old man." Randal slapped the phone into Amos's palm.

"Thanks. Now sit there and be quiet. Ms. Hodson, if he moves from that chair, you come let me know, okay?"

Julia nodded.

Amos walked into the office and closed the door. He tapped Randal's phone screen and texted Walter Burke.

What's your dad want with me?

Amos sat down and waited for a response. He

didn't have to wait long.

Where are you fucker?

Amos tapped his reply.

Let everyone go and I'll tell you.

A minute went by and then another. Amos sent another text.

??

Finally, Walter messaged back.

Who is this? Cops?

No.

Who r u?

Randal.

Bullshit. Tell me or someone gets hurt. Now. No joke. They get hurt it's on you. Countdown...

Amos jumped out of the chair, left the office, and went to the exit door. "What's going on?" Julia said. Amos saw Walter holding a phone up to his father's face. Willy took it, stared at the screen, and then put it to his ear.

The ringtone on Randal's phone started blaring Black Sabbath's "Iron Man."

"Shit." Amos lowered the volume.

Randal stood up. "Who's calling me?"

Amos watched Willy Burke's head move from side to side as he walked slowly around the courtyard. A hundred phone screens stared back at him.

"Hey, I said who's calling me?"

"And I told you to sit down and shut up. What part of those two things don't you understand?"

"And I'm tired of you bullying me. It's wrong. You're a teacher. You should know better."

Amos crossed the library until he stood directly in

front of Randal. "You have got to be kidding. You're tired of me bullying you? Mr. grope-a-freshman? That's rich."

"You're all talk. Give me my phone back or I scream."

Randal's phone vibrated. Another text had arrived. Amos read it.

Come to the courtyard now or we kill someone.

Amos held the phone up. "Go ahead and scream. The Burkes will be here in seconds. Remember, you're the one they want—not us."

"The door is locked. They can't get in."

Amos chuckled and grinned as he shook his head. "You poor dumb bastard. They're out there with Principal Dardner who also happens to have a master key. That means he can get into any room in the school. And that also means the only one keeping you safe from the Burkes right now is me."

Randal's shoulders slumped. "Oh."

"That's right—oh. So, at this moment, you have two choices, Mr. Risen. You can scream so the Burkes know where to find you or you can take a seat and shut up."

"Is that who's messaging you? The Burkes?"

"Yes, it is, and they want you in the courtyard right now or they're going to kill someone."

"Oh my god," Julia said. "What are we going to do?"

Randal's phone was ringing again. Amos went to the door and had another look outside. Willy Burke was no more than forty feet away with his back to him and a phone to his ear.

Julia's eyes were the size of saucers. "Don't be

stupid, Amos. Don't you dare answer it."

Amos took the call.

CHAPTER 10

10:42 a.m.

"**W**ho the hell is this?"

Amos shut the library office door before answering. "Someone who can help make sure this doesn't go badly for you and your boys."

"Why do you have Randal's phone? Where is he?"

"Listen closely, Mr. Burke. You need to let the people in the courtyard go."

"You a cop? The feds?"

"No, Mr. Burke, I'm none of those things. What I am is someone who gets it."

"What are you talking about? Get what?"

"I get why you're at the school today. I might not know the specifics, but I understand the motivation. I want to help."

"Help with what?"

"With getting your word out. You're clearly a man with something to say, right?"

"I don't need any help with speaking my mind."

"That's not entirely true, Mr. Burke. If law enforcement storms the school, they'll shut you up. Others will be hurt, including your children. I don't believe you're someone who wants to see that happen."

"Why should I trust you? I don't even know who you are. Is this a trick?"

"No, Mr. Burke, it most certainly is not. I have a contact with law enforcement outside. I know how close they're getting to coming in. We need to buy you some more time."

"And how the hell do you propose we do that?"

"I already told you. Let the people in the courtyard go."

"Are you in the school? Tell me. Tell me now or I shoot someone."

"I won't tell you—"

A gun fired. By the time Amos got up, Julia was already opening the door to the library office.

"You hear that?" she said.

Amos nodded. "Yeah." He started walking toward the exit with his hand over the cell phone.

"Are you talking to him?" Julia asked. "Willy Burke?"

"Go sit down."

"Not until you tell me what's going on."

Amos spun around. Julia stood with her arms crossed and her chin jutting upward. "I mean it. I want the truth. Why are you talking to Burke?"

"Hold on. Give me a second." Amos looked outside. Willy Burke was yelling into his phone as Dardner crouched in front of him on his knees. Amos put Randal's phone to his ear.

"The next one is the real deal," Burke shouted. "I'll shoot him in the head and it'll be your fault."

Amos cleared his throat. "You don't want to do that, Mr. Burke. Please, you have to listen to me."

"No, you have to listen to me. I asked you a question. Are you in the school?"

Julia poked Amos in the chest. "What's he saying?"

"Who's that?" Burke asked. "A woman?"

Amos covered the phone and leaned toward Julia with his teeth bared. "Go sit down."

Julia backed away slowly. "Thank you," Amos whispered to her. Julia gave him the middle finger.

"You still there, Mr. Burke?"

"Yeah. Now answer my question. Where are you?"

Amos took a deep breath. "I'm in the building."

"And you have Randal's phone. Does that mean he's with you? Because if you do—"

A helicopter flew over the school close enough it vibrated the floor beneath Amos's feet. Burke unleashed a long litany of curses and then ended the call. Seconds later, Amos's phone rang. It was Markley.

"Don't try to come in here," Amos said.

"That's not my call, Mr. Diaz. We heard gunfire. Is anyone hurt?"

"No, but there will be if you storm the school. I spoke with Burke myself. Don't push him."

"You did what?"

"I just had a conversation with Willy Burke. I'm trying to convince him to let everyone go."

"Jesus Christ, you're not a damn negotiator."

"I'm talking to him. He's talking to me. I'd like to keep the conversation going. So, you talk to whomever you need to talk to out there and have them stand down. Give me a chance to deescalate the situation."

"Have you lost your mind? You do know that if this goes sideways, you could be held liable, right?"

"I don't care about that. This is the best option. I really do think I can get Burke to listen to reason."

"And why is that?"

"Because he loves his sons. He doesn't want to see them harmed."

"He should have thought of that before he had them help to take a school hostage."

"I didn't say he wasn't confused."

"Confused? He's dangerous, Mr. Diaz. This isn't a classroom. It's the real world."

"Your views of my profession are duly noted, Officer Markley. Now, please make sure law enforcement doesn't attempt to enter the school."

"I'll do my best."

"Good. Thank you." Amos ended the call and turned around.

"Well?" Julia said.

Amos shrugged. "I'm going back into the office. Mr. Burke will call again soon."

"And what are we supposed to do?"

"Wait."

"For what?"

"For me to tell you what happens next."

Randal picked his nose with his thumb, rolled it between his fingers, and then flicked it onto the floor. "He's keeping us prisoner in here just like Burke is keeping everyone else prisoner out there."

Julia nodded. "He's right."

"No," Amos said. "He's not. I'm keeping you safe.

Big difference."

"Not from where I'm standing."

"Trust me. Don't trust me. Either way, I don't have time to care. Keep an eye on the door and on Mr. Risen. As soon as I know something new, I'll let you know."

"You mean you want me to help you keep Randal prisoner. Isn't that right?"

"That's fucking right," Randal said. Amos took a step toward him.

"You want to march yourself out the front door and say hello to the Burkes? Go ahead."

Randal didn't move. Amos nodded. "That's what I thought. See? I am keeping you safe, so stop being such an ungrateful little prick, or I might change my mind." He went back into the office, closed the door, and waited.

Nearly ten minutes passed before Burke called. The Glock pressed against Amos's lower back, so he put it on the desk in front of him.

"Hello again, Mr. Burke."

"Cut the mister shit. Just call me Willy."

"Okay, whatever you prefer."

"I prefer you tell me where Randal Risen is."

"I don't think that's your most pressing issue right now, Willy."

"No? Then what is?"

"Keeping that army outside from marching into the school and killing you and your sons."

"That's not gonna happen. I won't let it."

"I don't think you'll have much choice. As good a soldier as I'm sure you were, there's a whole lot more of them than you. And you saw the helicopter, right?"

"Of course. I told them no choppers. They didn't listen. They need to listen."

"Let the people in the courtyard go. Show the authorities you're not an unreasonable man."

"No way. I do that, and it's finished. You know I'm right. These people are the only thing keeping the guns outside."

"Then how about you let some of them go? Give the police a show of good faith. That'll buy you time to say what you want to say and still keep your sons safe."

"The principal stays with me. He's here until the very end."

"That's fine."

There was a long pause before Willy spoke again. "Okay, I'll do it. I'll let some of the kids leave."

"That's a very sound decision."

"Just one thing."

Amos closed his eyes. "What's that?"

"You tell me where Randal is. This whole thing doesn't work until he's standing in front of me."

"Mr. Burke, Willy, I can't do that."

"Why not?"

"Because I don't know where he is."

"Don't fucking lie to me. You have his phone."

"That's true. He left it here."

"And where is here?"

"I won't tell you that. Not yet."

"You're a liar."

Amos sat up straight. "My name is Amos Diaz. I'm a teacher here at Sky Valley High."

"I've heard the name. What the hell are you doing sticking your nose in all this, Mr. Diaz?"

"Just trying to keep people from getting hurt."

"You say Randal left his phone with you?"

"That's right."

"And why would he do that?"

"I don't know."

"How'd you know to message Walter?"

"I already told you I've been communicating with law enforcement. It wasn't difficult to pull his name up on Randal's phone."

"So, the cops told you all about me, is that it?"

"Some of it, yes."

"Can you see me right now? In the courtyard?"

Amos looked up and saw Julia and Randal sitting at a desk together outside the office. They were both staring him. "No, but I heard the gunshot and so did the authorities."

"Good. I wanted them to hear."

"If they hear another one, I'm certain they're coming in."

"I doubt that. There's local, county, state, and federal agencies out there right now. You're not the only one they've been talking to. I had an FBI agent on the phone just a little while ago. I got him pegged."

"Pegged?"

"Yeah, figured out. He's a classic cover-my-ass bureaucrat. He won't give the okay to enter the school until he absolutely feels he has no other choice, and that decision will likely have to come from someone above his pay grade. Especially since the media started showing up. I have time, Mr. Diaz. Likely more than you think."

"This isn't Afghanistan or Iraq. It's a public school in America."

"You don't think I know that?"

"Students are involved. Sooner or later, the authorities will try and save them from you."

"Maybe. That's why I'm taking your advice and letting some of them go. It's already happening."

Amos got up and nearly sprinted to the door. He looked out and saw a line of twenty or thirty students being led from the courtyard by Walter. The students suddenly stopped moving as Willy Burke walked slowly down one side of the line and then the other.

"What are you doing?" Amos asked. "Go on. Let them go. Don't go back on your word."

"Thank you," Willy said.

"For what?"

"For telling me you have a view of the courtyard. See you soon, Mr. Diaz. Let Randal know I'm coming for him."

The students started walking again. Amos backed away from the door as he reached behind him. The Glock wasn't there. He turned around, looked up, and locked eyes with Randal.

"What is it?" Julia asked.

Randal's head swiveled to the side as he glanced at the office. When he looked back at Amos he was grinning.

The race was on.

CHAPTER 11

11:04 a.m.

Amos tackled Randal football-style minus the benefit of helmet and pads. They both hit the floor in a tangle of arms and legs. Amos landed on top as Randal struggled to break free.

"Get off me you asshole."

"Not until you calm down and agree to go back to your seat," Amos replied. He was already short of breath. Seeming to sense Amos's growing weakness, Randal's squirming intensified. Amos clenched his fist, gritted his teeth, and delivered a glancing blow off the side of Randal's face.

"I said calm down."

Randal's hands encircled Amos's neck. His breath hissed out from his nostrils as he dug his fingers into muscle and cartilage. "I'm gonna kill you."

Amos gasped and coughed as his face took on a bluish hue.

"I warned you," Randal said. "You should have listened."

Amos toppled over. His head bounced off the side of the counter before he fell face-first against the floor. When he opened his eyes, he was on his back as Julia stood over him calling out his name.

"Amos, are you okay? Can you hear me?"

"Help me up."

Julia grabbed hold of Amos's arm and pulled. He leaned against the counter, took some deep breaths, and nodded.

"I'll be fine. Just need to clear the cobwebs. The little shit is stronger than he looks."

"Thank God. I thought you had a heart attack or something."

Randal was sitting down on the other side of the library rubbing the red mark on his face. Amos turned around and went into the office.

The gun was gone.

"I have it," Julia said.

Amos extended his hand toward her. "Good. Give it here."

"No. I'm keeping it."

"What? But it's mine. Hand it over."

Julia pointed the Glock at Amos. "I said no, and I mean it."

"Don't point that at me. You don't know what you're doing."

"Why? Because I'm a woman? How evolved of you to think so."

"No, because I assume you don't have any experience with weapons. Julia, it's dangerous. You could hurt someone. Please give me my gun back."

"Sit down."

Amos inched forward. Julia shook her head. "Don't test me. I've had enough of you and Randal literally at each other's throats. This library has far too much testosterone running through it right now. Until the authorities say we're free to go you'll stay in here, and he'll stay out there. Got it?"

"Don't be stupid. What if the shooters come in here? All three of us will need to work together to defend ourselves."

Amos's phone was ringing.

"I'll worry about that when I have to," Julia said. "Until then, you should probably answer that. Hopefully it's good news. We could all use some."

"Randal will try and get his hands on the gun. You know that, right?"

"Probably. I'm not stupid despite what you seem to think. Now answer your phone."

Amos took the call. "I don't know how you did it," Markley said. "And I don't care. Thirty-two students just walked out of the school alive and well. You have our full attention, Mr. Diaz. Clearly, Burke is willing to listen to what you have to say. Well done. We have a lot of very happy parents in the parking lot right now."

"I'm glad to hear those students are okay. How much time do I have to get more people released?"

"Maybe an hour. Two at most."

"That's it?"

Markley sighed. "I know it's not much, but the situation out here is getting weirder by the minute."

"How so?"

"Protestors are starting to show up. There's a couple dozen here already with the promise of a lot more to come from all over the state. The agent in charge, a woman by the name of Torrance—she wants to wrap it up before it becomes a complete circus."

"What in the hell are they protesting?"

"Guns."

Amos glanced up to see Julia running her fingers slowly down the barrel of the Glock. "Guns? I don't understand."

"The first few were anti-gun protesters. Then the gun rights people showed up soon after. Now both sides are facing off. It's all we can do to keep them from starting their own war out here. A CNN van just pulled in not more than five minutes ago. The story has gone national."

"Great."

"Yeah, just what we need, right? Which means what little time the feds are willing to give to see if Burke will release more hostages is now even more important."

Amos noted the time via the red digital clock on the wall. "I'll do my best."

"I know you will, Mr. Diaz. I'll check back soon. Good luck."

Amos put his phone away, took out Randal's, and prepared to call Burke but was stopped by the sound of the intercom coming on.

"This is Willy Burke. I want to let the cops outside know that the longer you give me to say my piece, the more people I'll let go. I just proved I'm a man of my word. I'd really appreciate it if you'd afford me more time to prove it.

"Okay, with that out of the way, we are still left with the reason why we're all here today. I left off explaining how my boy Walter was kicked out for confronting the disgusting shit of a child molester, Randal Risen. All Walter did was push him around a bit, which is a hell of a lot less than Randal deserves. The principal was sure quick to take Randal's side though. Didn't even give Walter a chance to explain what was really going on. He kept telling Walter how this was a 'zero tolerance' school and that violence of any kind was cause for immediate expulsion.

"Now just what the fuck does zero tolerance even mean? That specific situations aren't fully considered? That one set of circumstances might not be completely different than another? It's top-down dumbass bullshit is what it is. I have zero tolerance for incompetent imbeciles like Principal Dardner. How about that? And I have zero tolerance for child predator fucks like Randal Risen. Where's my justice? Where's the rules that benefit me and my needs?

"These schools don't prepare kids for reality. They're run by people who've never done anything and trap the students in a bunch of pretend nonsense. They tell you that you should feel ashamed and worried all the time. Everyone else is part of the problem and you have no choice but to be part of their solution. That you need to stop thinking for yourself. If you're white, you're wrong. If you're brown or black, you need their help because they say you can't do anything on your own. If you're a boy, you're a threat. If you're a girl, you're a victim. The textbooks are full of lies. The real history is being torn out and replaced by crap that just sets people up to be disappointed when reality hits them. All those hours sitting in classes being force-fed propaganda that's only meant to control people when they finally get out.

"I don't know about all of you but I'm sick of it."

Amos cocked his head. From the courtyard came a most unexpected sound. He got up, went to the door, and looked outside. A handful of students were nodding and clapping. Teachers scolded them to be quiet but they were ignored. Willy kept talking and the students kept clapping.

"I'm a dad. I'm a soldier. I mess things up. I try to do better. I know I'm not the only one but as many of us as there are, these days, we're the forgotten America. I like to get my drink on. I smoke a little weed. I crank up the Allman Brothers. I still salute the flag, scrape my knuckles, and work to get by. I like a woman with kind eyes and a killer ass. Does that make me an animal? Someone in need of rehabilitation? Nah. It just makes me a man, and if you have a problem with that, then I have two simple words for you.

"Fuck off."

Julia walked up to Amos. "What an idiot."

"Quiet," Amos replied. His head was still cocked as he continued to watch the students cheering.

"You don't actually agree with him, do you? The guy is nuts."

"Maybe you should take a moment to actually listen to what he's saying. I don't condone what he's done today, but I do understand the motivation."

"Really? Do you just understand, or do you also sympathize?"

"It's likely a little of both. Is that so wrong?"

"Yeah, Amos, it is. In fact, it's messed up. Burke is holding kids at gunpoint out there. The ones you hear clapping for him are likely scared to death and trying to get on his good side. There's nothing at all to sympathize in—"

Amos slammed Julia's arm against the wall hard enough that she cried out in pain. The gun fell to the floor. When she attempted to retrieve it, Amos shoved her away. When she tried to grab hold of his arms, Amos pushed her down, took the gun, and stepped back.

"Stop," he said. "We're on the same side. There's no need to be fighting."

Julia winced as she rubbed her wrist. "Says the man who just assaulted me."

"I'm sorry. I didn't mean to hurt you."

"Yes, you did. And you know what? I think that's the real you, Amos. You're a violent person—a bully. I didn't see it before, but I see it now."

Amos held up the Glock. "This is my gun. You shouldn't have taken it from me."

"And you shouldn't have brought it to school. This is a gun-free zone, remember?"

"Try telling that to the guns outside. I don't think they care. Or maybe they neglected to read the sign."

"Which makes you and them more alike than different."

"Well, shit, I guess you have all the answers. Now go sit down next to Randal."

Julia retreated to her chair. Amos heard a door close. His eyes narrowed as he watched another door open and Willy Burke emerge cradling an assault rifle. Dardner stood next to him holding a set of keys. Nine doors were left until they reached the library.

Amos turned around. "We need to hide—now."

CHAPTER 12

11:17 a.m.

"If they come in here, you're gonna shoot them, right?"

Amos and Randal were both standing chest to chest inside one of two closets in the library office. Julia was hiding in the other one.

"Let's hope it won't come to that," Amos said. "Now be quiet."

A lock turned outside and the entrance door to the library was opened. "Why's it so damn dark in here?" Willy barked.

"The librarian, Ms. Moore, called in sick today," Dardner replied. "It's likely nobody has been inside since the school day started."

"What's that over there?"

"That? Oh, that would be Ms. Moore's office."

Willy walked to the door, tried to open it, then turned to Dardner. "Unlock it."

"Yeah, the thing is, I'm not sure I have the key."

"What do you mean you don't have the key? You're the goddamn principal. You have all the keys."

Dardner shook his head. "No, not quite. Some of

the interior doors, well, they've had the same locks for years, long before I arrived, and it's not unusual for there to only be one set of keys to those rooms that only the applicable staff carry with them."

Willy used the tip of his pistol to scratch his temple. "Well aren't you a worthless wonder?"

"I'm sorry?"

"You should be." Willy pressed his face against the door glass, scanned the office, then backed away. "How many more rooms with views of the courtyard are there to check?"

"A few more?"

Willy scowled. "Are you telling me or asking me?"

"Uh, yes, I'm telling you there are a few more rooms."

"You sure about that? You better not be holding out on me. If we can't find where this Mr. Diaz is hiding Randal Risen, you're gonna be on the receiving end of my being seriously pissed and this is the wrong day for that."

"I assure you, Mr. Burke, I'm doing my very best to cooperate."

"Might have helped if you'd been that accommodating earlier instead of kicking my son out of school. Maybe took a few minutes to actually listen to his explanation instead of just assuming because his last name is the same as mine that he wasn't worth listening to."

"Walter's last name had nothing to do with his punishment. He assaulted a student. I had no choice but to follow the requirements of the district's zero—"

"Don't you fucking tell me about zero tolerance. Don't push off your own responsibility onto some bullshit policy. You called Markley. Markley called the cops. Everything that followed, everything about today, that's on you. You say my son assaulted Randal? Fine, but that was after Walter found out Randal tried to rape his little brother. Where's your zero tolerance for that?"

"Mr. Burke, if that's true, it's a matter for the police not a school administrator."

"The fuck it is. Walter tells you and you tell the cops and they go do their job and arrest Randal Risen. That's how it should have gone down, but instead, Walter tried to tell you and you shut him out and the cops escorted both him and me off school grounds. I have to wonder. If Walter was a black kid, would it have happened like that? I don't think so. No, people like you have your heads so far up your politically correct asses you would have laid out a red carpet for him and then turned on Randal quicker than flies on shit."

"I guess we'll have to agree to disagree, Mr. Burke."

"Only because you're too much of a coward to tell the truth. Walter is a poor white boy. That means he already had two strikes against him in your eyes. Pushing Randal around was a quick third and he was gone, no questions asked. You couldn't wait to kick him out, could you?"

"That's just not true."

"I guess we'll have to agree to disagree, Principal Dardner."

Dardner's smile was clearly forced. "Okay. Do you still want me to open up the other three rooms?"

"Yeah. Get moving."

When Randal tried to open the closet, Amos pushed him back. "Wait," he whispered. "Give it a few more minutes to be sure they're gone."

Julia didn't wait. She got out, gave the all clear, and then glared at Randal. "What did you do to Walter Burke's little brother?"

Randal shoved his hands into the pockets of his oversized jacket. "I didn't do shit and that's the damn truth. That kid says anything different he's lying."

Amos made sure the library's front door was locked. When he turned around, both Randal and Julia were looking at him. "What?"

"Well, do you think he's telling the truth?" Julia asked.

Amos shrugged. "Does it matter? The Burkes are the ones with the guns, so right now, their opinion is the only one that counts."

Randal's eyes flared. "I'm not lying. I didn't do anything to Waylon Burke. We hung out a little is all. He used to come over and play video games with me, so he could get away from his asshole of a dad."

Julia folded her arms across her chest. "Why would you want to spend time with someone so much younger than you?"

"I don't know. He was a good kid. He did what I told him."

Julia's eyes narrowed. "Yeah? Like what?"

"Oh, fuck off. Are you trying to say I'm gay for little boys?"

"Mr. Burke seems to think so."

"Yeah because he's crazy. I told you that already."

"Hey," Amos said. "Right now, none of this matters."

Julia looked like she wanted to spit in Randal's face. "The hell it doesn't. I'm the one who brought him back with me from the bathroom. I felt sorry for him only to find out he's the real reason for all the shit that's happened today. You should call Burke and tell him we have Randal. Let him have him so this can all be over."

Randal's eyes pleaded for an alternative before his mouth did. "No, please, he'll kill me. I promise I'll do whatever you say. I can go sit in a corner. I won't say a word."

"You sure sound like someone guilty of doing something wrong," Julia said.

Randal bit down hard on his lower lip. "I think he might have had a crush on me."

Amos shared a quick look with Julia. "Who? Waylon Burke?"

"Yeah. He started coming over more and more, eating dinner, staying the night. Then I had my first girlfriend and he got weird. When I told him I was too busy to see him as much, he started crying and saying how I was the only friend he had. That it wasn't fair how I was spending so much time with girls."

"What did you do?" Julia asked.

"I told him he sounded like a little fag. I didn't really mean nothing by it, but he freaked out. Totally trashed my room. So, I threw him out. That was like two years ago. Then out of the blue, his brother

Walter is in my face saying he's gonna kick my ass and how his dad is gonna kill me. I told the people in the school office about it because everyone knows how Willy Burke has PTSD, and that's when Walter got suspended. As soon as I heard gunfire this morning, I knew who was doing the shooting and who they were looking for. I ran into the bathroom and hid. That's the truth. Every bit of it. I swear."

Amos pointed to a corner of the library. "Go sit over there and be quiet."

"Huh?"

"You said if we kept you away from Mr. Burke, you'd go sit in a corner and wouldn't say a word, right? I like that idea, so get to it."

"You serious?"

"As a heart attack. Now go sit your ass down, face the wall, and keep your mouth shut."

Randal dropped his head, turned around, and did exactly as he was told.

"Huh," Julia said. "Looks like you actually got him to listen. Now what?"

Amos took out Randal's phone. "Now I try and get everyone else in the courtyard released."

Willy Burke answered on the second ring. "I'm looking for you, Mr. Diaz."

"I know. I want to offer you a proposition."

"Yeah? I'm listening."

"Let the rest of the people go and then you and I sit down together and talk."

"Where's Randal?"

"He's here. I'm looking at him now. I won't let you hurt him, Mr. Burke. That's now how this is going to play out. You need to stop worrying about Randal Risen and focus on keeping your sons safe. This could all go sideways very-very quickly. You let those people go and that'll buy us more time."

"And if I let them go, what stops the cops from marching into the school and shooting the place up?"

"I'm not going to let that happen either."

"For a teacher, you sure have a mighty high opinion of the things you can do."

"Mr. Burke, we really need to trust each other. I don't know you, but I do think you're a man of your word."

"That's because I am."

"Okay, then all I need from you is a promise to let the staff and students in the courtyard go and to meet with me to figure out where we go from there."

"I might very well be heading straight to hell before this day is done, Mr. Diaz. Are you willing to join me?"

"I'd prefer we find a different destination."

Willy chuckled. "Yeah, I imagine you would. A teacher like you has it pretty good. Guaranteed paycheck, all kinds of time off, a decent retirement. Shit, that sounds like paradise to someone like me."

"You'd be surprised."

"At what?"

"At how much I hate it."

"Really? Well do explain, Mr. Diaz."

"That's a conversation that would require more time than I think we currently have. Now if you let everyone go, we might manage to make some time for that kind of discussion. I'm certainly willing to try."

"I keep the principal—and you show me Randal."

"I'll agree to that after you let everyone else go."

"Done."

The call ended.

Amos went to the door, looked out, and waited.

"You pull this off, get all of us home safe, and you'll be a hero," Julia said.

"I don't care about that."

"No? Then what do you care about?"

"I'll tell you when I figure it out." Amos pointed at the glass. "Take a look."

The crowd in the courtyard was on the march. "Maybe we should try and sneak out with them," Julia said.

"Bad idea."

"Why?"

"Because I guarantee Burke is watching for that. He's letting all those people go. We can't jeopardize their safety for our own."

Julia's hand crept toward the door handle. Amos pulled it away. "I said no."

"There you go turning this place into a prison again."

"I'm just doing right by those people outside."

The courtyard was empty. Amos's phone rang. "Hello, Officer Markley. I thought you'd be calling."

"I don't doubt that, you glorious son-of-a-bitch. Burke let everyone go. They're all out here in the parking lot right now. It's one big happy reunion. Why aren't you with them? Where are you?"

"Keeping my word."

"What word?"

"You should know Burke still has Principal Dardner. Law enforcement is to remain outside the school."

"Is that coming from Burke or from you?"

"Does it matter? That's the situation."

"Mr. Diaz, are you being held against your will?"

"No, and Burke doesn't know where we're at—yet. Give me another hour and I think I can get Dardner released as well."

"Hold on. I'm going to run it by Agent Torrance."

Amos waited. Markley sounded out of breath when the call resumed. "Okay, you have your hour. When it comes to Burke, no one can deny you get results. How you get them, well, you'll have to explain that to us when all of this is done. Until then, I guess you just keep doing what you're doing and use that hour wisely."

"I intend to." Amos put the phone away. The courtyard remained empty. He turned around and found Randal still sitting in the corner staring back at him.

"Am I gonna die?"

"We all die," Amos replied.

"I mean today," Randal said. "Am I gonna die today?"

"I don't think so."

"Is that the truth?"

"Sure. Unless ..."

"Unless what?"

"Unless you don't do as you're told, like turning around, facing the wall, and being quiet."

Randal spun around. "Is that better?"

"Yeah, now be quiet." Amos took out the Glock and pointed it at the back of Randal's head.

"Amos, what are you doing?"

Amos lowered the gun. "Nothing."

"Put that away," Julia whispered. "It doesn't look like nothing."

"I was just making sure the safety was still on."

"Is it?"

"Yeah."

"Good. Now what?"

Amos stuck the Glock down the back of his pants and looked around the library. "Now we get ready for a visit."

"Visit? What are you talking about?"

"Willy Burke will be stopping by soon."

"How do you know that?"

Randal's phone was ringing. Amos took it out and looked at the screen. "Because he's about to be invited."

CHAPTER 13

11:39 a.m.

"You want me to come to you?"

Amos nodded while holding the phone to his ear. "That's exactly right, Mr. Burke."

"And why the hell would I do that?"

"Because it's likely the only way your sons get out of this unharmed with their futures intact."

"I already did what you said. I let everyone go."

"I know, and I thank you for that. It was the right thing to do."

"But you're still preventing me from locating Randal."

"No, Mr. Burke, you're not listening. Randal Risen is with me right now and I'm asking you to come here as my guest, unarmed of course."

"And my boys just walk out the front door?"

"That's my hope, yes. I believe I can arrange it with my law enforcement contact outside. I'll explain to him that you still have a few hostages including Principal Dardner. I'm willing to bet they'll give you a whole lot more time now that you've let most everyone else go. By doing so, you removed the imminent threat scenario. It's now a hostage situation on a much smaller scale. Law enforcement should be willing to wait that out for far longer. You've proven you're a reasonable man, Mr. Burke. That means you'll have more time to say what's on your mind and to argue your case directly to the American people. That's what you really want, right?"

"What I want is for my boys to stay with me. They're the ones who need to confront Randal face to face for what he did."

"Are you absolutely certain Randal is guilty of what you say?"

"You calling my boys liars?"

"No. I just think we need to be sure before putting that kind of accusation on someone. Was Waylon the only source of the allegation?"

"Why's that matter?"

"Didn't you tell me you've been accused of things you didn't do?"

Burke paused before answering. "Yeah."

"Well, I think we need to afford Randal a chance to give his version of what may or may not have happened between Waylon and him. Maybe it was all just a terrible misunderstanding."

"Did he talk to you?"

"Who?"

"Randal fucking Risen, who else? He already gave you his version, didn't he?"

"Some of it, yes."

"And?"

"Mr. Burke, I'd rather he tell you all that himself. That's the reason for my inviting you to join us in an environment that's safe for all parties concerned."

"Safe for all parties concerned?"

"I mean a sit-down where one person isn't pointing a gun at the other."

"Do you believe him?"

"Randal? I'm not sure. I do know he's very upset and scared by all this."

"I don't give a damn about that little shit's feelings."

"Okay, but what about the proposed meeting?"

"No guns?"

"Correct."

"And you promise Randal will be there?"

"You have my word."

"And I get to explain myself to the world?"

"If that's what you want to do then yes."

"You have access to the school's intercom system just like in the office?"

"I do."

"I'd like a few minutes to think it over, Mr. Diaz. That okay with you?"

"Absolutely, Mr. Burke. I'll wait."

As soon as Amos ended the call with Burke, he received another call from Markley.

"Sorry to bother you, Mr. Diaz, but the people out here are demanding a progress update."

"I'm working on it. That said, I'm pretty sure Burke is going to want more time. He's concerned about the safety of his sons. If he were to give himself up, he doesn't want them charged as well."

"Uh, those boys were clearly helping their father take a school hostage at gunpoint. That's not something the authorities will be willing to overlook."

"Then you need to convince them to do just that or this could still turn into something nobody wants to see happen. Burke appears to trust me just enough to at least consider laying down his weapons and letting the rest of us walk out of here alive."

"Did he tell you that himself?"

"Not exactly, but I believe it was implied, yes."

"Implied? You want me to go back to Agent Torrance with something you hope is implied?"

"Have I failed to deliver exactly what I promised yet, Office Markley? Nearly everyone who was being held against their will in the courtyard are now safely outside, correct?"

"Sure."

"Then make it happen. Give me more time."

"Give you more time? I thought you said it was Burke who needed more time?"

"You know what I mean."

"That's the thing, Mr. Diaz. I don't know. You seem to have taken a very keen interest in helping Mr. Burke stay safe."

"Are you accusing me of something?"

"You tell me. Are you?"

"Am I what?"

"Are you working with Burke?"

"Really? After everything I've done to get as many people out of this school safely, you want to come at me with that nonsense?"

Markley sighed. "Look, I'm only sharing some of what's being discussed out here. People are getting a little suspicious regarding how you've managed to get

Burke to do your bidding."

"That's crazy. They should be thanking me not accusing me. There are still people in danger."

"I know that, Mr. Diaz."

"Okay, then get me more time and don't contact me again until you do."

Amos put the phone away as Julia approached him from behind.

"That didn't sound like a happy conversation."

"It could have been better, but it could have been worse."

"Is Burke really coming here?"

Amos glanced up at the clock. "Maybe. I'm working on it."

"And you think that's a good idea?"

"If I can convince him to leave his guns and let everyone go, then yes."

"But what if he shows up and starts shooting?"

"He would have done that already. Nobody was hurt today, and then he let almost everyone go. Burke is a man with something to say, not someone who wants to see other people harmed."

Julia's brows arched. "And you know this how?"

"I don't know for certain. It's instinct. A feeling. Sooner or later, we all have to trust our gut, right?"

"The problem is, you're forcing the rest of us to trust you as well."

"You don't trust me? You think I'm a bad man? Even after I helped to get all those people released?"

"I'm not saying you're actually bad, Amos, but why are we still here after everyone else in the courtyard is gone? Why don't we just leave? Go out the fire escape door in the back and then run to the parking lot?" Julia grabbed hold of Amos's hands. "I want to go home."

"If we open the fire escape door and Burke is in the main office, he'll know exactly where we are. Maybe we get to the parking lot before he reaches us and maybe we don't."

"But you're actually inviting Burke here. How is that any safer?"

"He's coming without any weapons."

Julia glanced down. "And he doesn't know you have a gun."

Amos nodded. "That's right. He's bringing Dardner with him, which means we can make sure he also gets out of here safely."

"I thought you considered Dardner an asshole?"

"Sure, I despise him as a principal but that doesn't mean I want to see him hurt. Besides, he saved us when he told Burke he didn't have a key to the library office. Dardner had to know we might have been hiding in there. We owe him."

"He wasn't lying to Burke when he told him he didn't have the key. As far as I know, Ronda really is the only one who can lock and unlock the office from the outside."

"So, you don't think Dardner was actually trying to protect us?"

"I don't know. He did announce that 'code white' thing, which I'm pretty sure was meant to let staff know something was up and to get outside as quickly as possible."

"Yeah, exactly. We owe him."

"And what's the plan if Burke does show up without his weapons and Dardner in tow?"

Amos tilted his head toward the office. "I'm going to give him some time on the intercom to speak his mind. That's what seems most important to him right now. Let him vent and then we all walk out of here together."

"Just like that?"

"Sure, why not?"

Julia's eyes narrowed. "Burke knows he'll have access to the school's intercom system when he gets here?"

"Yeah, that's what I told him. Why?"

"But he doesn't know we're in the library, right? You haven't told him our location yet?"

"That's correct. I wanted time for us to prepare to help ensure everyone's safety."

"Amos, Burke already knows where we are. You just told him."

"No, I didn't."

"Yes, you did. There are only two locations in the school with access to the intercom system—the main office and the library. Dardner knows that and I'm almost positive Burke knows it now as well."

Amos ran a hand over his head. "Shit."

There was a firm knock on the library door. Amos pointed toward the fire exit. "We need to get out of here."

The color drained from Randal's face. "Willy Burke is right outside," he said.

Amos didn't turn around. "I know. Let's go. Follow me."

The second knock was much louder. As soon as Amos pushed the fire exit partly open, an alarm sounded. He motioned for Julia and Randal to hurry as he pushed the door all the way open and then looked up to find the business end of a rifle a foot from his face.

It was Walter Burke. Amos backed away slowly.

"You all need to sit down," Walter said. He had to almost shout, so his voice could be heard over the alarm. "My dad wants to have a word."

Walter looked past Amos and smiled. "Hello there, Randal. It sure is nice to see you again."

CHAPTER 14

11:59 a.m.

"You already had the key to the library," Amos said. "Why'd you bother with trying to sound like you were breaking the door down?"

Willy stroked his beard. "Because it got all of you all to scatter like rats. Let you know right off there wasn't gonna be any easy escape."

"You said no guns."

"No, you said no guns."

"We had a deal, Mr. Burke."

"That deal was you leading me to Randal. You didn't do that. I found him myself. What I'd like to know now is if you three have been hiding out in here all along? Were you actually inside that little office over there earlier?"

Amos nodded. "We were."

"So, the principal was lying to me."

"No," Dardner said. "I really don't have the key to the library office. I never lied to you, Mr. Burke. You asked that I call in the fire alarm code to get it shut off, so we didn't have to sit here screaming at each other to be heard, right? I did that as soon as you asked me, just like I've done everything else you've wanted from me."

"He's telling the truth," Julia added. "The librarian is the only one with the key."

Burke grunted. "That right? Now who are you again?"

"Julia Hodson. I'm the art teacher."

"What's an art teacher doing hiding out in the library? Where's the librarian?"

"I was in here visiting with Mr. Diaz. The librarian, Ms. Moore, is out sick today."

"I already told you that, Mr. Burke," Dardner said.

Burke jammed his gun into Dardner's shoulder. "Did I ask to hear from you? No, I didn't. Sit there and shut up." His head swiveled toward Amos. "And why were you in the library today, Mr. Diaz?"

"I was covering for Ms. Moore during my first period prep."

"What's a prep?"

Amos shifted in his chair, careful to keep the back of his shirt pulled down over the Glock. "Teachers get one period a day without students, so we can prepare lessons, correct papers, that sort of thing."

"And you get paid for that time even though you're not teaching?"

"That's right. We're still working."

Burke went back to stroking his beard. "Uh-huh. Sounds like quite a racket to me. How many hours are you at the school during a typical work day?"

"It varies."

"Give me the damn average."

"Seven."

"And how many of those hours are you actually teaching?"

"Five."

"Five hours? Wish I could get paid a full wage for part-time work like you."

"There's more time involved than just teaching, though," Julia said. "There's lesson planning, grading, supervising; some teachers put in a lot more time than a typical eight-hour day."

Burke smiled. "And how much time does an art teacher put in?"

Julia scowled. "It depends."

"Do you have to grade as much work as a science teacher, or an English teacher, or a math teacher?"

"No, probably not."

"But you all get paid the same?"

"There's a pay scale we follow, yes."

"What's that pay scale based on? Performance?"

"No, it's primarily based on years of experience and the amount of continuing education a teacher has." Julia straightened in her chair. "I have a master's degree, so I make more than someone who doesn't."

"You have a master's degree in art?"

"No. It's a degree in education technology."

"Like computers and stuff?"

"Yeah, basically."

"And does that degree actually make you a better art teacher or just an art teacher who makes more money?"

"I'm sorry?"

"How much did the master's degree cost you?"

Dardner attempted to interrupt. "What does this

have to do with—"

Burke glared at Dardner. "I told you to shut up. It's her question. Let her answer it."

Julia cleared her throat. "About $6,000 dollars. I did it online. It took me two years."

"Uh-huh. And how much more do you get paid after getting that degree in how to turn a computer on?"

"Almost $10,000 a year more."

Burke's eyes got big. "So, you spent $6,000 dollars to get $10,000 more every year for as long as you teach? That's one hell of a return on investment."

"That's right. It's a master's degree. It's more education. A teacher should get more money for doing that."

"But the degree doesn't really make you a better art teacher, right?"

"I didn't say that."

"You didn't deny it."

Julia's nostrils flared. "Why are you picking on me?"

"I'm not. I'm just trying to understand this nonsense that's packed into all these goddamn schools we're forced to send our kids to. You're an art teacher who's paid the same or more than an English, math, or science teacher even though you pretty much admitted you don't have to correct nearly as much homework or tests or spend time preparing lessons as those other teachers do. And then you go and get a master's degree that doesn't have anything to do with what you're teaching, and you're rewarded with another ten grand a year for as long as you're a teacher. Little lady, all due respect, but that's insane."

"Are you jealous? Is that what this is about? The guns? The hostages? The threats? You resent the money I make?"

"Disappointed is more like it."

"You want to talk about disappointment? How about coming to work and having to hear gunshots and kids screaming? That's real disappointment, asshole."

"You're mighty lippy for an art teacher, Ms. Hodson."

"You asked me questions. If you don't like the answers I gave, that's your problem."

Burke nodded. "Yeah, I suppose so. Seems we've gotten a bit off track." He pointed at Randal. "You're the little shit my boys and me are here to see. Isn't that right?"

Randal started to cry. "Please don't hurt me, Mr. Burke. I didn't do what you think I done. It wasn't like that."

"If you didn't do what I think you done that would make my son Waylon a liar. Is that what you're calling him? A liar?"

"I'm saying I didn't do anything wrong."

"Yeah? You two used to spend a whole lot of time together."

"I suppose. Waylon liked to hang around me. We played video games is all. It was never nothing weird. I'm no pervert. I promise."

Burke grabbed hold of Randal's oversized jacket and pulled him out of the chair. "Your promise don't mean shit to me, boy. It's truth-telling time, so get to it. What did you do to my youngest?"

Randal's crying turned to wailing sobs. Snot ran down over his lips as his entire body trembled. "I didn't do nothing, Mr. Burke. That's the truth. I swear I never did anything to Waylon. I never would. We were friends and then we weren't. That's all. That's all it ever was."

Burke glanced at Waylon. "Sure seems like he's calling you a liar, son. You have anything to say about it?"

Waylon was looking down when he answered. "Randal hurt me. He wasn't my friend."

Burke's grip on Randal tightened. "See? You hurt my boy, you disgusting piece of shit. Now you're gonna pay."

"Wait!" Amos stood with his hands up. "Just hold on. You really don't want to do that, Mr. Burke. Remember? You also came here to share a message. If you harm Randal, that won't happen. If I don't check in with my law enforcement contact, then there'll be a whole lot of guns marching into the school very soon. When they do, they'll likely kill you and your sons. It's clear you care deeply for your children. I don't believe you'd ever want to see them harmed in any way."

Burke dropped Randal into his chair, stepped sideways, and stood in front of Amos. "This all started because my sons were harmed." He pointed down at Randal. "One was harmed by him. The other was harmed by this place when he tried to make things right for his little brother."

"I understand, Mr. Burke. You want to talk about this place, correct? How about we focus on that? We can go into the office and talk it over—what you might want to say to everyone else outside listening."

"I don't need some teacher trying to put words into my mouth. I know my own mind. I can speak for myself just fine."

"Of course. I wasn't implying anything more than you being afforded the opportunity to do just that. Randal will be here waiting. Your sons can remain out here to keep an eye on him. You have the guns, Mr. Burke, which means you also have all the power—at least in here. That power will be taken away, though, if you choose to harm Randal now."

Burke wagged a finger at Amos. "You got one thing right. I'm in charge here. I do have the guns, which means I do have the power."

"Your real power is the opportunity to get your message out. I want to help you to do that. C'mon, let's go into the office and get started."

Burke looked down at Dardner, Julia, and Randal. "You stay right here in those seats." He nodded to his sons. "Any trouble from them, feel free to shoot. You have my permission. I won't be too long." Burke followed Amos into the office.

"Close the door," Amos said.

"Okay," Burke replied. "Now what?"

"Now we sit and talk for a bit."

"The only talking I'm gonna do is over the intercom so everybody can hear what it is I have to say. That's what your promised me. Turn it on."

Amos sat facing Burke. "Not yet. I'm going to wait to hear from my law enforcement contact and then you and I are going to have a conversation before we get the intercom going."

"You seem to think you're the one giving orders. Let me make it very clear. You're not. I'm the one with the gun, remember?"

"It's hard to forget with you holding it in front of me like that. Have a seat, Mr. Burke. It won't be long."

Burke grabbed a chair and fell into it. Dark bags had made a home under his eyes.

"You look tired," Amos said.

"I've been tired for a very long time."

Amos nodded. "Me too, Mr. Burke. Me too."

The two men sat staring at each other, waiting and watching.

Both were armed but only one of them knew it.

CHAPTER 15

12:32 p.m.

"**M**ore time? Mr. Diaz, these people aren't playing out here. They are highly armed and ready to go at a second's notice. Do you understand?"

"I do understand, Officer Markley, which is exactly why you need to give us more time. Everyone inside the library is okay. We're talking things out and hopefully soon, we will be reaching a resolution to this entire misunderstanding."

"Misunderstanding? What the hell are you talking about? The Burkes took a school hostage. There's no misunderstanding about that."

"I'm speaking to their motivation."

"No, you're speaking out your ass."

"Be that as it may, we need more time. If the authorities come in here shooting, people will be hurt and that'll be on all of you. If a little more time prevents lives from being lost, how is that a bad thing?"

"Mr. Diaz, you sound like you're working with the Burkes."

"I'm working to keep everyone safe. That's it."

"And Principal Dardner is safe?"

"I already told you he is. I have no reason to lie about that. Now go tell Agent Torrance to stay back."

"You do remember I'm just a school resource officer, right? You want me to go up to the federal agent in charge and tell her what to do?"

"Yes."

"Mr. Diaz, I never would have thought you could possibly be such a huge pain in my ass."

"I don't mean to be. I'm just doing my best to make sure cooler heads prevail."

"Is that really it? That's all you're doing?"

"I have to go, Officer Markley. Mr. Burke is going to say some words soon. Stand down until he's done doing so. Thank you for your help. I sincerely mean that."

Amos looked up. Burke appeared impressed. "You got a knack for that kind of talk," he said.

"What kind of talk?"

Burke shrugged. "Convincing people to see things your way. You should have been a politician. Got the right skin for it."

"Skin?"

"Yeah, that mocha tint of yours. It's all the rage these days—minority this and minority that. It's no time to be a poor white man, that's for sure."

"I don't think it was ever a good time to be poor, white or otherwise."

"Yeah, well, it's even worse these days. Are you even full nigger?"

Amos's face tightened. "Could you please not use that term?"

Burke blinked several times like he'd just realized something for the first time. "Oh, hey, I don't mean nothing by it. Just an expression. I served with plenty of ni— black folks when I was in the service and they used that word a hell of a lot more than I ever did."

"I'm mixed race."

"See? I knew it. Man, all you need to add to it is to say you're a homo and it's a politically-correct hat trick. You could be the next goddamn president. I bet you got your college for free, didn't you?"

"Excuse me?"

"Don't play dumb. I'm talking all that affirmative action bullshit. They must have been throwing all kinds of money at you. Someone like you gets the 'we are the world' types all hot and bothered. You know I'm right."

"I did the work. I earned my degree."

Burke smiled knowingly. "But did you have to pay for it?"

"I was awarded scholarships based on merit not the color of my skin."

Burke threw his head back and laughed. "That's a pile of horseshit. I read an article a while back about this very thing. It said that the Asian kids were being penalized on that SAT test for being too smart and working too hard. Colleges were complaining that too many of them were being granted admission. They wanted more diversity, which of course is just a fancy word that means more blacks and browns and whatnot. Now imagine that. Here are these little Asian kids minding their own business and doing their best and the colleges they want to get into bend them over and fuck them right in the ass because they're not the right kind of minority. That's the system we're living in today, and it's not right. Tell me I'm wrong."

"Is that the message you want to share on the intercom today?"

"Yeah, that and more. Not yet though."

"You want to wait? Why?"

Burke placed the pistol on his lap. "What's your story, Mr. Diaz? You married? Have kids of your own?"

"I was married once. No kids."

"Why's that? The no kids I mean."

Amos's chin dropped onto his chest as he stared at his shoes. "I was unable to get my wife pregnant."

"Ah, shooting blanks, huh?"

Amos didn't reply.

"I'm sorry to hear that. So, you say you were married once. Is that why your wife left? She wanted children?"

Amos looked up. "I don't want to talk about it."

Burke rested his hand on the gun. "I wasn't asking what you want, Mr. Diaz. I want to hear your story. Where's your wife?"

"She's dead."

Burke's brows lifted. "Dead? Really? You kill her?"

Amos clenched his jaw. "Of course not. It was a car accident."

"Were you two still married when it happened?"

"No. We divorced a year earlier."

"Did you still love her when she died?"

Amos took a deep breath. "I told you I don't want to talk about it."

"And I told you I'm not asking. It was your idea to

come in here. Your idea to have a conversation. So, let's fucking converse. Why'd she leave you?"

"I never said she left."

"You didn't have to. I can see it all over your face—the rage. It's still there. That woman messed you over good, didn't she? I'm not judging. Been there myself, remember? My wife left me too. She's still alive, though, bless her selfish bitch of a heart. Shacking up with some fireman a thousand miles from here. Hardly talks to her own kids. How messed up is that? I do my best, but you know having a mother that takes so little interest in them has to hurt those boys. Make them feel like they're just shit that the world wants to scrape off the bottom of its shoe. You should be grateful you didn't make any babies with the ungrateful cunt who left you."

"Yeah, maybe."

"Was your ex friends with the people you work with?"

"No, not really. Stacy didn't respect this job. She thought teachers were overgrown kids who wanted a redo of their own school days. My colleagues knew her, but she made it very hard for them to like her."

"Do they know she's dead?"

Amos shook his head. "I never told them about the car accident."

"Huh. You're kind of complicated, aren't you?"

"I'm not sure what you mean."

"Married. Divorced. Wife dies but you don't tell the people you work with. Come to school with a gun."

Amos's mouth dropped open. "What?"

"Yeah, that gun you have on you. The same one

Waylon saw you carrying earlier this morning when you two ran into each other in the courtyard."

When Amos went to reach behind him, Burke aimed his pistol at Amos's chest and shook his head. "No-no-no-no. Don't be stupid. Keep your hands in front of you. We're conversing, remember? There's no need for violence. I got no plans to shoot you. How about you afford me the same fucking courtesy? Can you do that?"

"Sure, I can do that."

"Good. So, let's keep talking."

"What about?"

"Oh, I don't know. How long did it take for you to find out your wife was cheating on you?"

"Why do you think she was cheating on me?"

"You have that look."

"Look?"

Burke nodded. "Yeah, the look of a man whose been burned by the fires of infidelity."

"You make it sound almost poetic."

"I don't have much in the way of a formal education, Mr. Diaz, but I'm not a stupid man."

"I already suspected as much."

"That a compliment?"

"Probably as close to one as you'll get from me."

"Okay, I'll take it. Now tell me about your marriage falling apart."

"What's this about? Why the personal questions?"

"I'm doing what you said we were going to do," Burke said smiling. "Just two emotionally damaged men with guns having a talk."

"I thought you just wanted to speak your mind

over the intercom."

"Yeah, that'll happen soon enough. Right now, I'm trying to figure out who the hell you are."

"And why is that?"

"Need to know if I can trust you."

"If you're pointing a gun at me, I'll give you the simple answer. It's no."

Burke held out his hand. "Give me yours and I'll put them both out of the way. Sound fair?"

"Will I get it back?"

"Sure, when we're done."

"You do realize this requires me to trust you, right?"

"That's pretty much the point, Mr. Diaz. It'll help us both to trust each other. Now reach behind you slowly and then hand it over."

"And if I refuse?"

"Then I'll have to take it from you. It would be a big mistake if you think I won't or that I can't. This situation, this thing we're doing right now, it'll feel a whole lot more comfortable knowing one of us isn't possibly seconds away from drawing down on the other. So, man up and give me the gun."

Amos took out the Glock, paused, and then handed it to Burke.

"There," Burke said. "That wasn't so hard."

"Now you," Amos whispered.

"Despite what you might think I really am a man of my word. See?" Burke took both guns and put them on a shelf behind him. Then he cracked his knuckles and rolled his head from side to side. "Now go on and tell me what happened with your marriage, Mr. Diaz.

What did that woman do to you?"

"Before I get into all of that, I'm going to need a drink."

"Water?"

"No, not water—a drink. There's a bottle of vodka here in the desk drawer."

"Are you shitting me?"

"Here, I'll show you."

Burke leaned forward. "Do it slow. No tricks."

Amos brought out the bottle and put it on the desk. "It belongs to the librarian. Given the circumstances I don't think she'll mind."

"Well, look at that. Teachers bringing vodka and guns to school and yet I'm the guy everybody is so damn quick to call a criminal."

"Want some?"

"Hell yes," Burke answered. He took the bottle, tilted his head back, had a long swig, and then handed it to Amos who did the same.

"So," Amos said. "You want to know what happened between me and my wife? I don't know why but after the already bizarre nature of this day, who cares? I'm sharing vodka shots with the man who took my school hostage. How much more bizarre can it get from here?"

"Have you told anyone else?"

"No. You're the first."

Burke leaned back in his chair and crossed his arms. "Okay, let's hear it."

Amos took another sip from the bottle. "My relationship with Stacy was never ideal. We were married under false pretense. I thought she was pregnant. That alone, given the strain of not being able to have kids later, was more irony than I cared to have to take. Stacy always wanted more. At first, she treated me a bit like an exotic pet. She was tall, blonde, attractive, and outspoken. I was dark, reserved, educated, someone devoted to my job as an educator.

"She came to loathe the few social events she attended with my fellow teachers. Her eyes were always looking elsewhere, even when we were the only two people in the room. As the years went on, we talked less and less but still tried to have children. I even suggested adoption. She refused that option. When she accepted a position in the accounting department at a car dealership, we barely saw each other at all. One time, I had the day off and surprised her with a basket lunch. As soon as she saw me walk into the dealership, I knew it was a mistake. She told me to never again come to her place of business without first asking if it was okay."

"No offense, Mr. Diaz," Burke said, "but your wife sounds like a total bitch."

Amos gave him a pained smile. "Wait, it gets better. Stacy was getting home later and later. When I asked her why, she ignored me. We had a terrible fight. Not a physical one. She was still my wife and I honored that. But things were said, and we slept apart. In fact, we never slept in the same bed again. A few weeks later, I opened a credit card statement that was addressed to her. There were only four charges on the statement—all taking place in the evening and from the same hotel.

"I went there the next night and waited. Stacy drove up alone an hour later. I watched her go inside and was about to follow her when another car pulled up and parked almost directly in front of me. I recognized the driver. He was a former student."

Burke's hand partially covered his mouth. "Oh shit."

"I won't say his name. It doesn't really matter. He had graduated three years earlier. I found out later he was a salesman at the dealership that was owned by his grandfather. I have no doubt Stacy saw him as an end to her own means. He came from money—money she wanted to be a part of. She was also a lot older than him, which I'm sure made it more exciting for them both.

"I followed him to the room and then paced the hall outside for a while wondering what I should do next. I was about to turn around and go home when I noticed one of the hallway maintenance closets was partly open. Sitting on a shelf inside was a keycard. I took it, went back to the room, and stood outside the door for what felt like forever. There was a 'Do Not Disturb' sign hanging from the handle. You could hear what was going on inside."

Burke's eyes narrowed. "Don't you dare tell me you pussied out."

"I didn't. I scanned the card, unlocked the door, and went inside. It was dark. They were both so busy enjoying themselves they didn't realize I was there. I heard everything. Every moan, every grunt, every impassioned declaration to God above. I stood frozen in the blackness as a former student made love to my wife. Finally, no longer able to just stand and listen, I turned the light on.

"They were on the bed. The young man was on his back. Stacy was on top of him but facing me. There was a second or two of panic in her eyes, but that passed quickly. She just smiled and kept going while I watched. I heard him ask about the light. She said not to worry about it. He had Stacy in a way I never had—and she loved it. That was clear. It was as if I wasn't there and every time her hips thrust down, I felt a piece of who I thought I was dissipate like a shadow giving way to the sun. Both their movements became more urgent, more demanding. Stacy was this feral thing that was finally set free the way she gasped and groaned and dug her fingers into the sheets. She arched her back until her hair fell over the young man's chest as she unleashed this low, guttural howl. She climaxed, and he soon followed.

"I didn't realize I was crying until a tear fell onto my shoe. I wiped my eyes and looked at Stacy. She was smiling. The young man finally realized I was in the room and went to get up, but Stacy told him it was fine. She said there was nothing to worry about because I wasn't really a man. He called me Mr. Diaz like I was still his teacher. Told me he was sorry. Stacy told him to shut up and then told me to get out."

Amos paused.

"What did you do?" Burke asked.

"Do? I got out. I went home. I waited. Stacy didn't return for two days and when she did, I was handed a manila envelope with divorce papers. She'd been planning to end the marriage for some time. I said I wasn't selling the house. She said she didn't want it. Even then, after all I had seen, I tried to reason with her. I suggested counseling. Stacy laughed. She said it had been over between us since the day we started. Although we were nearly the same age, she called me an old man and said being with me was like living in an open grave that was just waiting for the dirt to come along and cover it back up."

"What's that even mean?"

Amos shrugged. "I don't know, but it was effective. She finally managed to piss me off enough that I grabbed her by the shoulders and shook her. Not hard, but it was all she needed."

"Needed?"

"Stacy called the police. Claimed I had assaulted her. She did that knowing full well it could jeopardize my teaching certificate. I'd lose my job. I begged her not to press charges. She asked me how much I was willing to give her to keep quiet. I told her she knew I didn't have much to give on a teacher's salary. It didn't matter. By the time she left that day, I had promised to send her half my check for the next five years."

"Are you telling me that not only did the bitch get caught messing around on you but then she also shook you down for more money? And the guy who was sticking it to her was a former student of yours? And all you did was cry about it? What the hell is wrong with you, man?"

"Mr. Burke, there isn't nearly enough vodka left in that bottle to cover all the potential answers to that particular question."

"Is everyone else at this school as messed up as you or are you the exception? And to be so goddamn visual about it. It's like listening to soft porn."

"You said you wanted to hear what happened to my marriage and you wanted the truth. I told you—and that's not even all of it."

"There's more?"

"Indeed. After the divorce, Stacy started asking me for even more money. Then she decided she did want her half of the house. When I said no, she threatened to tell people I had beaten her and that she could still file assault charges against me because the statute of limitations hadn't yet run out."

"You really picked a winner with her. The gift that keeps on giving."

"That's one way of putting it."

"Let me guess. You gave her more money."

"No. In fact, I didn't give her another dime."

"Why not?"

"Remember? The car accident. Stacy died. They both did."

"Both? You mean—"

Amos's eyes twinkled as he nodded. "Yeah. Her lover was in the vehicle with her. She was driving. They were killed. I guess sometimes good fortune comes in twos." Amos glanced up at the guns. "Isn't that right, Mr. Burke?"

CHAPTER 16

12:55 p.m.

"Huh," Burke said. "Funny thing is now I don't know what to say."

"Sure, you do. What you said earlier was perfect. Build on that. Share your experience. Tell your truth. Expose the ridiculous nature that is this monstrosity we call public education. That's why you came to the school this morning isn't it?"

Burke shrugged. "I guess. I don't know. Fact is, I'm tired. Look at my boys out there holding guns on those people. Maybe ...maybe this was a mistake."

"What? Need I remind you that's Randal Risen sitting out there? From what you've said already, he's far from an innocent."

"Now that I've seen him, I'm not so sure he did what Willy says he did. I know my son. I know how he looks when he thinks he's putting something over on someone. As soon as he saw Randal, he had that look. Willy wants to scare Randal, but he doesn't want to hurt him."

"If that's all he wanted, then I'd say he's succeeded, because Randal looks like he could shit himself at any moment."

Burke buried his face in his hands. "I don't know what I'm doing here. I think I really fucked things up. I'm going to jail for this. Who's gonna take care of my boys?"

Amos touched Burke's shoulder. "Let's try not to worry about that. A lot can happen between then and now. You have a voice, Mr. Burke, and you do have something to say." He placed the vodka bottle on the desk. "Have another drink. We're going to be fine."

"What's this we shit? And why do you want to help me so much?"

"Nobody has been hurt today. Frightened, certainly, but not hurt. You're a father wanting to defend his sons against a system that so often is so wrong about how it goes about its business. I heard your words over the intercom this morning. Please believe me when I tell you I really heard them, understood them, and I sympathize with the message."

Burke tipped the bottle back and then scowled. "I've already forgotten half the shit I said. I was running on adrenalin and just wanted to get my hands on Randal. Now that I have him, I think I'd rather just let him go."

"Forget about Randal Risen. Just focus on what you'd like to tell the world."

"The world doesn't give a shit about what someone like me has to say to it. Besides, it isn't listening. It never has."

Amos got up and turned on the television monitor that was mounted in a corner of the office. "That's where you're wrong, Mr. Burke."

A young, blonde, very serious-looking local news reporter dressed in a form-hugging blouse and skirt stood outside the school talking into a microphone as a red-lettered Breaking News alert scrolled underneath her. Burke glanced at the television screen, took another drink, and then set the bottle down slowly as his mouth dropped open.

"There's got to be a thousand people in that parking lot—maybe more."

Amos nodded. "More is right. I'd estimate close to twice that number. They're lined up and down both sides of the road. Everything you say into the intercom, the media and all those people will hear and pretty soon, a whole lot more will be listening as well."

With his eyes reflecting what he was watching on the screen, Burke pointed at the television. "Turn it up," he whispered.

The news camera panned the large crowd as the reporter described two fiercely opposing sides that had formed outside the school. One side was pro-gun rights. The other side wanted guns banned. People sneered, taunted, flashed their middle fingers, and threatened to kick the other side's ass. The reporter reminded viewers that although the shooters had already let almost everyone go, some hostages remained inside the school, including at least one student, two teachers, and the school principal. She went on to share that the governor had condemned the violence and indicated his hope that the conflict would be resolved as quickly and as safely as possible.

Burke took another drink and shook his head. "Fucking politicians. They use words while managing to never say anything. And why are they calling us shooters? We never shot anyone."

"You did fire your weapons inside the school," Amos said.

Burke poked his chest several times. "I shot a few rounds—me. That was it. My boys didn't shoot anything. Their guns are just for show. I made certain of that before we came here."

"What do you mean?"

"Nothing," Burke answered while glancing at his sons as they stood guard over Julia and Randal. He sighed, shifted in his chair, and stroked his beard. "This going to happen or what?"

"You mean the intercom?"

"Yeah, the fucking intercom. Show me how to turn the damn thing on. Let's get this over with."

"Do you know what you're going to say?"

"No, but, whatever."

Amos shut off the television. "No, not whatever, Mr. Burke. This is important. You should say what you mean and say it clearly to the people out there who need to hear it."

"You sound like you know what I'm going to say more than I do. Maybe you should be the one to talk."

"I'll deliver my message later. This is your time."

"You have a message?"

"We all have something to say. Every one of us. It's just that so few are given the chance to do so. Your chance is right now. You can't afford to waste it. If not for you, then for your sons."

Burke pushed himself up from the chair. Amos stepped in front of him. "Get out of my fucking way," Burke snarled.

Amos reached behind him and brought out his Glock. "I don't think so, Mr. Burke. Please sit."

Burke looked up to where he had put both weapons. They were no longer there.

"That's right," Amos said. "I took yours as well. So, let's try and communicate with one another without all the threatening macho bullshit."

"What the hell do you think you're doing? You don't pull a gun on a man like me. That's likely to get you killed."

Amos smiled. "Thanks for the warning. I'll take my chances." The smile vanished. "Now sit your ass down."

"You and me both know you won't ever pull that trigger. You're a fucking teacher. A paper clip. A guy whose day is divided up by the ringing of a goddamn bell."

"That's good stuff. The rage, the disgust—save it for the intercom."

"I'm not your goddamn slave. You want me to say something? Say it yourself and in the meantime, you will get out of my way."

"I'll kill your children. Look me in the eyes and tell me I won't."

"Don't you ever threaten my boys."

"I just did, Mr. Burke. It's clear you don't fully appreciate the situation you find yourself in so let me take a moment to explain it to you. You have two sons standing on the other side of this door. They have weapons—but not loaded ones. You said it yourself. You made sure the guns they're carrying were just for show. I couldn't possibly know that, though, could I? So, I would be well within my right to shoot them, and you, dead. And that's what is going to happen if you don't start doing exactly what I say."

Burke's entire body tensed as he gripped the side of the desk. Amos shook his head. "Don't do it. You'll be dead long before you reach me. Then I'd have no choice but to do the same to your sons. No, Mr. Burke, the most prudent thing for you right now is to sit down and speak into the intercom. Share with the world your frustrations over how society has ignored you and your family, how the school system neglected to treat you fairly. That is your truth. That is what needs to be heard by others."

"You're insane," Burke said as he lowered himself into the chair.

Amos shrugged. "Perhaps but it doesn't matter. You're going to do what I ask, or everyone dies."

"I remember you even though it was almost twenty years ago. I had your class. You failed me."

"No, you dropped out of school. I gave you an incomplete. You failed yourself."

"So, you do remember."

"I remember most everything, Mr. Burke. That's likely part of my problem. It's tough to move on when so many details of your past grow heavier with each passing year. The greater the burden of memory, the more difficult it is to forgive and forget."

"What the hell happened to get you so twisted up inside? Was it all your wife?"

"Stacy? No. She was just another brick in the prison of my own making. You ask what happened? Life happened. Disappointment and so much terrible regret for things I never did happened. Everything about my entire existence since I started teaching feels the same. The only thing that changes is time and it keeps pushing right on past me. That regret I feel is a poison ball in the pit of my stomach. It's eating me up inside. I can feel it right now. Whatever potential I had, whatever I might have become, it's all gone. Like you, I too have failed myself. There's nothing left. That is, until your arrival this morning."

"Me?"

"We have so much in common. The world has disappointed us in so many ways. You were no doubt pushed out of school as much as dropped out, leaving you to join the military and then forcing to fight wars in far-off lands for reasons that likely remain as mysterious and confusing to you now as they were then. And what did you return to? The very same system that had spit you out before. You scrape to survive, father two children, only to see them abused as you were. Our lives now are empty remnants of that abuse. We still breathe, eat, shit, sleep, wake, but is either of us truly alive?"

Amos answered his own question as he shook his head slowly. "No, we're not. We died a long time ago, didn't we? The exact date isn't important. It happens gradually, an accumulated absence of joy, love, contentment. We're not alive, but we are still aware, and it is that awareness of our own sadness, regret, and rage that drives people like us to do things others judge as monstrous. But we are not monsters. We are broken and forgotten vessels that wish to know there is something more than merely day-to-day existence. We desire to live, to love, and to be accepted, not for what others would have us be but rather for who we have always wanted to be."

"Jesus," Burke muttered. "What have I gotten myself into?"

"It's going to be fine as long as you do what I ask of you."

"Speak into the intercom?"

"That's right. And stick to your story, your experiences. I am not to be part of your message. Do you understand?"

"Sure."

"I mean it, Mr. Burke. You try to message the authorities about me in any way and I'll put a bullet into the back of your head and then do the same to everyone else, starting with your sons. Do you understand?"

"Yeah, I understand. You're telling me what to do just like everyone else I've ever known. It's the same old shit: school, the military, government, cops, and now you."

"Are you ready?"

Burke glanced down at the phone. "How do I turn it on? It's different than the one in the main office."

"Just hit zero-nine on the keypad and that will activate the intercom."

"You mind if I have a bump first? I need to clear my head."

"Bump?"

"Yeah, just a snort or two is all."

"You mean drugs?"

Burke placed a vial of powder on the desk. "It's Adderall."

"For ADHD?"

"That's right," Burke said while tipping the vial over and tapping out a short line onto the pad of skin between his thumb and index finger and then snorting it. "It was prescribed to Waylon a couple years ago. The school counselor said it would help him focus."

"Why are taking your son's medication?"

Burke had another hit before putting the vial away. "I first used it in the military. We'd grind it up and take it while pulling guard duty. Half my battalion was on the stuff. It allowed us to stay awake for days at a time, but the coming down can be brutal. I don't use nearly as much as I did back then. Just a little here and there when it helps—like now. Besides, Waylon don't even need it. They say he has trouble focusing? He's a fucking kid. Give me a break."

"I need you focused, Mr. Burke."

Burke's eyes sparkled as he moved his head up and down rapidly. "Exactly, that's why I took some. Now I'm focused for you like a goddamn laser, man. Whew. Oh, yeah. I'm ready-ready-ready. Just hit zero-nine?"

"That's correct. Press those two numbers and you're live. The stage is yours."

Burke clenched his teeth tightly together and inhaled so the air hissed between them. His hand trembled slightly as it hovered over the keypad. He glanced up at Amos.

"And this will keep you from going postal on my kids? I have your word on that?"

"Yes, you have my word."

The heel of Burke's foot started to tap against the linoleum floor. He stared at the keypad. His hand was no longer trembling.

"Okay. Fuck it. Let's do this."

CHAPTER 17

1:11 p.m.

"**S**ending my kids to school is like killing them slow. That's how I really feel, and if any of you out there don't like hearing it, you can just kiss my ass because I don't give a damn what you think about me or us or anything else.

"I remember holding the hand of my oldest on his first day of kindergarten. We were both kind of scared. He was scared because it looked all big and different and there were all these faces he didn't know and new rules to learn. I was scared because his being there was just another reminder of how fast time was going by. He was born, learned to walk and talk and now school had started. Soon, it would be girls and wanting to drive and then he'd be out of the house and I'd be sitting there with memories and old age creeping in and way too much time to start wondering how many days my own life had left.

"What I wasn't prepared for was having to witness how school took from my boys far more than it gave. They used to smile and laugh all the time. I don't think I've heard Walter laugh in years. It's like that part of him was ripped out by this place. Why is it teachers are always going on about saving the world when we can't even save ourselves? Have any of you met a teacher who's actually happy with what they're doing? I sure as hell haven't. Sure, they walk around smiling and nodding but I've seen enough to know when something is real and when it's fake, and let me tell you, there's a whole shit-pile of fake in places like this. Teachers are some of the most miserable little motherfuckers you'll find."

Burke arched both brows as he looked over at Amos. Amos nodded and gave him a thumbs-up.

"Okay, so my showing up here with a gun today wasn't the right thing to do. I get that. I understand a lot of things most folks don't think I understand. I may be simple, but I'm not dumb. No sir. And as for my boys, they're both smart. A lot smarter than their old man. Smart enough to deserve to be treated better than the people running these schools have treated them. They also know when they're being pushed aside and kicked down, and we're all goddamn sick and tired of that.

"My oldest, Walter, his grades aren't so bad. He's done okay despite all the crap the teachers and principals have thrown at him. He likes writing and music, and he's pretty good at both. Good enough he started thinking about college. He took some pamphlets from the counseling office a few months back. Brought them home to read and then he made an appointment with the school counselor to discuss his plans for the future. That's what he's supposed to do, right? Think about what he wants to be and all that shit. He makes the appointment, shows up two days later, and the counselor isn't there. The secretary—Walter tells me this later—the secretary looks at him like he's a runny hairball the cat just yacked up on the rug. Her nose crinkles when she asks him what he wants. He made a damn appointment but she's apparently just so disgusted by his existence or something that an appointment doesn't matter. Walter tells her to fuck off and leaves. Yeah, I suppose he shouldn't have said that, but can you blame him? I sure as hell don't.

"He's not a quitter though. He makes a second appointment. Now, I didn't know about any of this at the time. This was Walter taking care of his own business. A lot of kids wouldn't know the first thing about how to do that. They got their heads so far up their phone's ass, they haven't seen real daylight in years.

"Walter shows up for that second appointment and this time, the counselor is there. She gives him that same wrinkled nose look the secretary did the other time. It's a look that says to someone they don't belong. That they aren't worthy to be considered for help. And they're saying this to a kid—my kid. What gives them that right? Who do they think they are?

"So, this counselor talks with Walter for all of two minutes and in that time, she explains how he's probably not suited for college. She brings up how his grades aren't quite good enough. His test scores aren't quite good enough. He's not quite good enough. Walter gets a little upset and then the counselor, quick as water running off a frog's ass, calls the resource officer in to escort him out of her office. It was all one big fuck-you to a kid who just wanted a little help with planning his future.

"All right, fine. That's how things go. Life isn't fair. People are assholes. I know all about that, believe you me. But then something happens. This something involves another student. He's a real shithead, a scumbag, the kind of someone worth less than the spit in your mouth. I won't say his name. I don't need to call him out. Fact is most everyone will likely know who I'm talking about anyways, especially if you've bought the skunk weed he sells most days in the parking lot. He's a Mexican kid. His folks aren't even legal. I've met them. Not bad people but don't hardly speak a word of English. They snuck into the country a few years ago. Their son, well, he's a piece of shit. A wanna-be thug who started selling drugs shortly after he got here. None of that matters to me. I really mean that. Where people come from, how they choose to live—whatever. Do your thing, man.

"Here's the problem though. This kid, the teachers and the principals and the counselors, they all call this drug dealer a dreamer. And you know what? He's been bragging about how colleges are throwing all kinds of money at him. He's in this country illegally, he deals drugs, and he gets to do something my son is told he can't do—go to college. And get this. The other kid, the dreamer, his grades suck. That's no secret. He hardly shows up to class and when he does, he's high most the time. Everybody knows it. The kids, the teachers, the principal, and no doubt that bitch of a counselor knows it too. So, I'm looking at this situation as a parent, and I'm wondering why my son is told he's not good enough while the pot-peddler is told he's more than good enough. How the hell does that make any sense? It doesn't. No way. No how.

"We know what's going on here. It's discrimination. One student is white. The other is brown. The white one, my son, is told to fuck off. The brown one, the illegal one, the one who's overseeing a little parking lot criminal enterprise, is given the golden ticket so that all of you who are part of this bullshit system can pat each other on the backs and say how much you all care about protecting the world from the evil white man.

"Yeah, let's go there. Let's talk race—white, black, brown, whatever. When I was a kid, it wasn't an issue. And when I was in the military, it wasn't even a thought. We were all soldiers. We were all Americans. Any of you dickless fucktards who want to call me a racist because I'm pointing out the racism that runs our schools today can go on and fuck off. Racism is real, but it isn't the racism we were taught about not so long ago. No sir. If you're a parent of white children in America today, you have to deal with everyone telling them they should feel guilty for their whiteness. That they should be punished. That they are less than kids whose skin happens to be darker than theirs. That if they don't just accept how they are second-class because of their whiteness, then they are the problem and not the solution. This is the kind of crap they're being told. This is the shit they are forced to read in the textbooks.

"And if you're white and male? Forget it. You're

the worst of the worst. Speaking of which, I'm really not getting off track here. This is all related. This is all part of what's going on in our schools today. And about that white male thing, do you know what my youngest boy's teacher asked him to do on the first day of class? He was told to declare his pronoun. When Waylon told me about it, I didn't even know what that meant. His pronoun? I mean, what the hell? He's a he or a him because he's a boy goddammit. So, here's this teacher, she's telling everyone in her classes they have to declare their pronoun. Jesus H. Christ, like being a kid isn't confusing enough, now we got to go and throw that kind of shit at them?"

Burke chuckled. "You want to know what Waylon's first answer to that question was? He said he wasn't a fag. Man, you would have thought he'd started World War Three. The principal was called in, the district's parent-teacher mediator wrote up this remediation plan that included Waylon having to spend four hours cleaning up garbage on the school grounds. And for what? Giving an answer to a question that never should have been asked? An answer they found unacceptable? It's all so ridiculous. What the hell happened to common sense in this country? Since when did having kids identify their genders in school become more important than teaching them how to read and write? I can't be the only parent who thinks all of this is batshit crazy. Can I?

"The high school is even worse. Walter told me about a school assembly they had recently. This person shows up. It's a man in a dress, high heels, makeup, a wig, the whole nine yards. He's there to share his story about how he identifies as a woman. He talks about how tough it was growing up and being scared of who he really was and how only now, after all these years, does he feel safe enough and confident enough to be the woman he was born to be. Okay. Uh-huh. Whatever, dude. You want to get your freak on? Have at it. Just don't put that shit in front of school kids and try to convince them it's normal. Walter said teachers were applauding this guy. Some of them had tears in their eyes. They were all nodding to each other like it was the most amazing story they'd ever heard. It was one big drama circle-jerk. I did some asking around. I wanted to know how much we paid for that fella in a dress to show up. The district didn't want to say, so I looked him up on the Internet. I found his website. He travels all over the country to tell his story—for a price. That price is $7500. A man puts on a dress and wig in front of a roomful of school kids, talks for about an hour about how brave he is for identifying as a woman, and pockets $7500. Got to hand it to him, that's quite a racket. Makes me wonder what my own dress size is; $7500 for an hour of talking? Sign me the hell up.

"Which brings me to what happened that got Walter kicked out of school without so much as a second's worth of consideration by that prick of a principal who runs this place. Like I said before, Walter was just doing right by his little brother by dealing with Randal Risen directly. Burkes don't go to the cops. We handle shit ourselves. Isn't that what men used to be taught to do? Anyways, he confronts

Randal and Randal denies it and there's some pushing and shoving and a punch or two was thrown. No big thing. Boys being boys kind of stuff. Except Randal has Principal Dardner suspend Walter just like that. Randal goes and says Walter has been harassing him for weeks, that he calls him names and makes fun of him. He hit every damn red button on the district's zero tolerance policy and got Walter kicked out. These kids aren't stupid. They know how to play the system. But here's something I didn't tell any of you about yet—something the principal told me right before I marched out of this hellhole with my son. He looks at me and says my son is a bigot and bigotry has no place in public education. We were in his office, just me and him. Walter was waiting outside the door. And then he goes on to say how bigotry is learned and that I've done my son a terrible disservice by passing on my own history of hatred to him.

"History of hatred? Who the fuck does Dardner think he is talking to people like that? I wanted to kill him then and there. That's no joke. Those soft wet eyes of his looking at me like I was nothing more than a booger to be flicked away and forgotten. Yeah, he's sitting in the other room from me right now. How easy it would be to get up and go kick the shit out of him. Too damn easy. No sport in thumping a weak-ass little bitch like that. I'll let him be for now so long as the cops stay away. You hear me? Give me space to think. Don't come in here trying to be heroes. That'll only get people hurt."

Burke smacked the top of the desk. "I'll tell you what. And I just decided this right here and now. I'm willing to die today. That's right. I'm willing to fight and die for what I got to say. Are any of you? I see what's on the TV. I know there's a whole lot of you out there listening in the parking lot, and I got to think some of you really do understand what I'm getting at with all this. I don't mean the guns and the hostages. Those things are just, well, stuff that happened from there to here. No, what you and I do have in common is that we're pissed off, we've had enough, and we ain't gonna just sit down and take this shit no more. Am I right? Let me hear you. I said am I right?"

Both Amos and Burke looked up at the sound of shouting coming from outside the school. Burke snorted another line of Adderall and then clapped his hands together. "That's what I'm talking about!" he said. "I can hear you. Keep it going, man. There's a whole lot more of us than these schools will admit. In fact, we might just be the majority out there—parents who want some basic fucking common sense returned to places like this. What do you say?"

More cheers erupted. Amos pointed to the phone. "Turn it off," he whispered. "Press zero-nine again."

Burke scowled and gave Amos the middle finger. Amos pointed the Glock at Burke's head. "Turn. It. Off."

Burke rolled his eyes, poked the numbers on the keypad, and let out a long sigh. "Make up your goddamn mind. You say you want me to talk, so I talk. Now you're pointing a gun at me and telling me to shut up. What gives?"

"You're high. You're not thinking clearly. I don't want to see anyone harmed."

"I'm just talking. How's that going to get anyone hurt?"

"Mr. Burke, you just told the authorities you were willing to fight and die. What do you think they're response will be to that kind of threat? Let me tell you. They will come in here and mow us all down—your sons included. Is that what you want?"

Burke got up. "I already said that isn't gonna happen. There's too many eyes and ears on this thing now. You heard them all cheering out there. I already let everyone in the courtyard go and now I'm just talking. You really think the cops would shoot up some kids and teachers because they don't like that I'm speaking the truth about the shit that goes on in places like this? Shut up with that nonsense."

"I don't have an issue with anything you said except the willing to die part. That's dangerous. That will get people hurt."

Burke stared down at Amos as he leaned toward him. "I am willing to die for my right to say what I want to say. If that doesn't fit with whatever game you have going on here, that's not my concern. You don't like my words? Then take a seat and speak your own."

"What about your sons?"

"Stop bringing up my boys. Don't try and use them to control me. Yeah, I'm wise to you, Mr. Diaz. You played the kid card one too many times."

"Mr. Burke, this is no game."

"Everything's a fucking game." Burke took a step toward Amos. "Everyone has an angle, including you. Now put that fucking gun down before I shove it sideways up your ass."

"Don't move. Stay there. I mean it."

Burke looked past Amos. "I want to check on Walter and Waylon."

"That's fine. Go ahead." Amos stepped aside. Burke walked out of the office and then slammed the door closed behind him. He gave each of his sons a quick hug while they proudly exclaimed how great he had sounded on the intercom. Randal asked to use the bathroom. Waylon told him to hold it. Dardner and Julia sat side by side on the couch. Julia turned her head, stared into the library office, and locked eyes with Amos. He nodded to her. She looked away.

The library phone rang. Amos picked it up.

"Hello?"

A deep-voiced woman answered. "Who am I talking to?"

"This is Amos Diaz. I'm a teacher here at the high school."

"I know who you are, Mr. Diaz. I've spoken at length with Resource Officer Markley. I'm Special Agent Torrance. Is it safe for you to speak?"

"Yes."

"And why is that?"

"I'm sorry?"

"I mean how is it that Willy Burke was just using the very same phone I'm now speaking to you on? What happened to Mr. Burke?"

Amos put the Glock on the desk and then sat down so the others in the library couldn't see him talking. "He's here. He's fine."

"Fine? You're saying the man allegedly holding you hostage is fine?"

"I meant, uh, he's here. He's still here."

"In the library with you now?"

Amos licked his lips. "No. I mean yes. He's in the library but I'm in the office. The door is closed. He can't hear me."

"So, Mr. Burke left you alone?"

"That's correct."

"Why would he do that?"

"Again, I don't understand."

"Mr. Diaz, I'm asking why your alleged captor is willing to leave a hostage alone and unsupervised. That doesn't make any sense."

"He's not alleged. He's here and that's what he's doing."

"I need you to confirm for me who is in the library with you at this time. Are you ready?"

Amos switched the phone to his other ear and then used the back of his hand to wipe the sweat from his glistening forehead. "Okay."

"I'll say a name and you simply reply yes, or no. Understood?"

"Got it."

"Randal Risen."

"Yes."

"Willy Burke."

"Yes."

"Walter Burke."

"Yes."

"Waylon Burke."

"Yes."

"Julia Hodson."

"Yes."

"Doyle Dardner."

"Yes."

"Is that it, Mr. Diaz?"

"Correct. Besides myself, those are the only other ones here in the library with me."

"Very good. I have just one more question for you at this time."

Amos gripped the phone so tightly his knuckles were white. "Okay."

"Are you in any way working with Willy Burke?"

Amos rocked back in the chair like he'd just been hit with an electric cattle prod. "Why would you ask me such a thing? That's ridiculous."

"Just doing our due diligence, Mr. Diaz. Please don't take it personally."

"Well, I do. We're all very frightened in here."

"I understand and assure you we are doing our best to see this resolved as quickly and peacefully as possible. That's what you want, isn't it?"

"I have to go. Burke is coming back. I'll let Officer Markley know when it's safe for me to speak again. Goodbye, Agent Torrance."

Amos ended the call. The Glock was on the desk directly in front of him. He grabbed hold of it, brought it slowly to his lips, opened his mouth, and slid it inside. His upper teeth scraped against the cold metal as his finger wrapped around the trigger.

It would be so easy.

No more pain.

No more disappointment.

No more having to remember.

Just the weightless embrace of cold, dark

nothingness.

Amos closed his eyes, tilted his head back, and smiled.

CHAPTER 18

1:39 p.m.

Nothingness was interrupted by another call from Markley. Amos pulled the gun out of his mouth and grabbed the phone.

"What?"

Markley's tone made it clear he wasn't pleased. "Don't you dare 'what me,' asshole."

Amos gave as good as he got. "And fuck you too."

"Listen very carefully, Mr. Diaz. Something's not right in that library, and everyone out here knows it. What the hell are you up to in there?"

"I have no idea what you're talking about."

"Fine, play it like that and you're going to get yourself a nice long prison sentence—or worse."

"I'm sorry, Officer Markley, would you please explain what this is about?"

"How are you able to always be picking up your phone if you're being held hostage? Where is Mr. Burke?"

"He's here, he's armed, and that's exactly what I already told Agent Torrance. What more do you need to know?"

"I know what you told her. She's already briefed everyone. That's why I'm calling you now."

When Amos didn't respond right away, Markley shouted into the phone. "I'm calling you because Agent Torrance suggested it. I'm calling you because you're a stupid sonofabitch who's about to get a lot of people killed. I'm your last chance, Mr. Diaz. I'm the only thing standing between the authorities storming the school right now and their willingness to wait and see for just a little bit longer. Do you really not understand what I'm telling you?"

"It seems you believe the shit is about to hit the fan."

"Yes, that's exactly what's about to happen. You confirmed that Burke is leaving you alone and unsupervised. That does not sound like the actions of someone holding people hostage. What it does sound like is two people working together."

"Agent Torrance already presented that accusation. I'll tell you the very same thing I told her. It's ridiculous."

"Is it? You're hiding something. Agent Torrance and her colleagues are certain of it, and their patience has run out. Did you really think you'd be able to fool the FBI? This kind of thing is what they do. It's the air they breathe."

"If the FBI is so certain of that, then why are you calling me?"

"Because Agent Torrance requested it."

"Right, which also means she isn't nearly so certain as she's telling you she is. Look, I'm sitting inside the library office with the door closed. The

Burke family is just a few paces away. They all have guns. I don't understand what you or the FBI or anyone else finds so confusing about that scenario. I'm a victim and yet you seem determined to make me complicit in the events I and others literally find ourselves hostage to."

"Let me speak with Ms. Hodson."

"Julia? Why?"

"Because I need to confirm that she is in fact safe."

"You don't believe me when I say she is?"

Markley's answer came after a long delay. "No. Let me speak to her."

"I'll have to ask Burke if that's okay. I have no idea if he'll allow it."

"Get her on the phone—now."

"I'll do my best. It might take a few minutes."

"Fine. I'll wait."

Amos put the call on hold, opened the door, and motioned for Julia to come inside. Burke followed her into the office. "What is it?" Julia asked.

Burke's eyes narrowed as he noticed Amos holding his phone. "Who are you talking to?"

Amos ignored Burke and looked only at Julia. "Markley wants to speak with you to make sure you're okay."

"Oh," Julia said. "Sure, I'll talk to him." She held out her hand to take the phone. Burke reached around her and pushed the hand down.

"Hold on. I didn't say you could talk to anyone."

Amos gently pulled Julia toward him. "Mr. Burke, I think it's best you allow Ms. Hodson a chance to calm the nerves of all those armed people in the parking lot who are very close to entering the school. She'll be brief. They just need confirmation that's she hasn't been harmed."

"What? By me? I haven't hurt nobody besides smacking that principal around a little."

"That's right," Amos said. "And that's all they wish to confirm at this time. If they don't hear from her right now, I think it will be a matter of minutes before they break down the door."

Burke scowled as he shook his head. "Nah. They won't be doing that. Not yet. We still have time."

"Time for what?" Julia said while looking from Burke to Amos.

"Ask him," Burke replied. "He seems to think this is his operation now. We're all just along for the ride. Isn't that right, Mr. Diaz?"

Julia moved away from both men. "Amos, what's he talking about? What's going on?"

"He's talking nonsense. Ignore him. Mr. Burke, can Ms. Hodson and I please have a moment alone?"

"Are you asking me or ordering me?"

Amos shrugged. "Call it whatever you want as long as it gets you to leave."

"Sure, I'll leave but then I'm coming back, and you and I are gonna have a real serious conversation. You hear me?"

"Yeah," Amos said. "I hear you."

Burke left. Julia stayed. Amos held up his phone. "Keep your comments brief. He'll likely try and gather more information from you. Avoid saying anything that might set off Burke. I'm certain I'm very close to convincing him to give up and let us all walk out of here."

"He seems to think that's not his decision."

"That's his attempt to divide us. Just ignore it. Need I remind you his boys are the ones on the other side of that door holding rifles?"

"Where's Burke's gun?"

Amos straightened his shoulders and stuck out his chest. "I have it."

"What? How? Why?"

"It's like I just told you. He's very close to letting us leave but the difference between that and a much more tragic scenario is razor thin. We must proceed with great caution."

"You're avoiding giving me a real answer. Why would Burke give you his weapon? That makes no sense. He said you thought you were in charge. Are you?"

"Of course not. It's more a matter of my being able to convince him to try and save his sons and that he needs my help in order to do that. He's very unstable you know — highly medicated."

"Drugs?"

Amos nodded. "He's snorting his son's Adderall. I watched him do it."

"So, for now, I'm just supposed to let Officer Markley know that I'm doing okay? Is that it?"

"Yes. It'll give me the time I need to see this situation resolved safely. Burke already let the people in the courtyard go. I'm confident he's very close to letting us go free as well."

Julia held out her hand. "Okay, give me your phone."

"Remember, keep your answers brief. We don't need something getting back to Burke that will agitate him."

"Yeah, got it."

Amos hesitated. "Are you sure you understand? We have no room for error, Julia."

"Do you want to stick your hand up my ass and move my mouth for me too? I think I can manage to talk to someone on the phone without you telling me exactly what to say. You're sure not doing yourself any favors in getting me to believe Burke isn't right."

"Right about what?"

Julia poked Amos in the chest. "That you really are the one in charge here. Maybe it's not him keeping us hostage. Maybe it's you."

"That's insane."

"Insane? You took my phone. You took Burke's gun. Now you're trying to tell me what to say to Markley. It sure feels like you're calling all the shots."

"Keep your voice down. We don't want Burke thinking there's a problem."

Julia folded her arms over her chest and cocked her head. "Are you going to give me the phone or not?"

"I will after you promise not to say something stupid."

"What? Like the truth?"

When Amos rolled his eyes, Julia made a grab for the phone. Her shoulder struck him in the stomach as the phone fell from his hand and clattered onto the floor.

"Stop it," Amos snarled as he reached under the

desk with one hand while attempting to push Julia away with the other. She scratched at his face. Amos closed his eyes, turned his head, and shoved her as hard as he could. His fingers found the phone as Julia fell backwards. She struck the wall with a heavy thump and then slid to the floor.

Amos looked down at the phone and saw the call with Markley was still on hold. Julia wasn't moving. She lay on her side with her mouth and eyes partly open.

There was blood—a lot of it.

"Jesus," Amos whispered. He glanced out at the others in the library. The Burkes had their backs to him. Dardner and Randal were both sitting and reading magazines.

Amos knelt beside Julia and put his hand on her shoulder. "Hey, are you okay?"

More blood pooled beneath Julia's head. Amos looked up and saw the busted frame of an old pencil sharpener that was bolted to the wall. The thick plastic cover was broken into several jagged sections like a row of shark teeth. One of the sections was missing.

Amos felt the back of Julia's head and found the piece of hard plastic embedded deep into the soft space where the top of her neck merged with the bottom of her skull. The blood that oozed from the wound did so more slowly until finally it stopped.

"Oh, no."

Amos began to put his hand over his mouth and then realized it was wet. He stared at his fingers while using his thumb to slowly rub the blood between them. He got up, opened one of the closets, and stuffed Julia's body inside it. The door wouldn't stay closed because she kept falling forward, so Amos removed the laces from one of his shoes, wrapped it around her neck, and then tied it to one of the coat hooks at the back of the closet.

That worked. The door remained shut. Amos found some towels by the sink and used them to wipe the blood off the floor. After he was done, he dropped the towels into the closet and then washed his hands in the sink. He dried them off, held them up to the light, and nodded. They were clean. All was nearly well with the world once again.

Amos picked up the phone and resumed the call. Markley responded immediately.

"Hello? Who am I speaking with?"

"It's me."

"Diaz? I thought you were going to allow me to speak with Ms. Hodson?"

"I'm sorry, Officer Markley. Burke won't allow it. I tried my best to convince him. That's what took so long."

Amos kept staring at the closet door. "I assure you she's fine. I'm looking at her right now."

"Mr. Diaz, we had a deal. You said I would get to communicate directly with Julia."

"No, I said I would try, and I did. Burke said no. I still think I can convince him though."

"Let me guess. You just need more time."

"That's right. None of us here are in any immediate danger. If the authorities try anything right now, that will most likely change things for the worse.

Burke has already let almost everyone go. I'm confident he's almost ready to let us go as well."

"Goddammit, Diaz, we really needed to confirm with Ms. Hodson that she was okay. Tempers are stretched thin out here. There's been ten arrests already and more are imminent. Oh, and keep that sonofabitch Burke off the intercom. His support is growing. I counted at least fifty pro-Burke signs in the parking lot in the last hour alone. We're having a real tough time keeping a lid on all this shit. That's a big reason why the authorities want this wrapped up sooner rather than later."

"I assure you nobody wants that more than me. If Burke changes his mind about allowing you to speak with Julia, I'll let you know immediately. You have my word."

"You sure you can't make that happen now?"

"I'm sorry. She's not available to speak per Burke's direct orders. Speaking of which, he's coming this way now. I have to go. Goodbye, Officer Markley."

"Stay safe, Mr. Diaz."

Amos continued to stare at the closet door. "I intend to. Thank you."

CHAPTER 19

2:02 p.m.

Amos had lied to Markley about someone coming into the office. Burke remained with the others in the library. The youngest, Waylon, had fallen asleep with his rifle resting on his lap. His father sat cross-legged on the floor smoking a cigarette. Dardner was in a chair looking at a wall while Walter stood a few feet away looking at him.

There was something else in the library office with Amos though. He heard a gasp, some scratching, and then a heavy thump. The closet door that held the body opened a few inches. Amos stood frozen as he watched a hand emerge with fingers that curled inward like claws.

"Hello?" Amos slowly raised the Glock.

The entire closet shook. There was another gasp, a choking sound, and then a long sigh. A familiar voice whispered from within.

"Help me."

Amos crept toward the closet, gripped the door, flung it open, and then cried out as a mass fell forward and smacked against the hard floor. The same hand

Amos had watched come out of the closet reached out and tugged on the bottom of his slacks.

"Please help me."

Julia Hodson was alive.

Amos slid his foot back from her hand and then realized it was holding the piece of pencil sharpener plastic that had been sticking out of her lower skull just a few minutes earlier. Her other hand gripped the shoelace he had used to tie her neck to the coat hook inside the closet.

Julia turned her head, opened one eye, and glared at Amos. "Why are you just standing there?" Her voice was stronger despite the blood that continued to ooze from the wound at the back of her head.

Amos went to help her up and then stopped. Julia closed her eyes and appeared to lose consciousness. Amos put the gun up to her ear. "You're supposed to be dead," he mumbled. He took another deep breath and then another like a child trying to gather the courage to jump into the deep end of the pool. His hand was steady where it held the Glock inches from Julia's head. His finger pressed against the trigger. Behind him the office door opened.

"What the hell is going on in here?"

Amos slid the gun into the front of his pants. "She hurt her head."

"That right?" Burke leaned over Amos's shoulder and looked down at Julia. When he saw the back of her head, he winced. "Ouch. How'd that happen?"

Amos pointed to the wall. "She fell backwards and hit the pencil sharpener."

"What's that mark around her neck? Looks like

she was trying to hang herself."

"I'm not sure," Amos said with a shrug.

"She don't look so good. Might need a doctor."

Amos pulled Julia up toward him and then wrapped his arms around her chest. "Help me to get her into that chair."

Burke pushed the chair toward Amos. Julia's eyes fluttered open briefly when she sat down and then closed again.

"Hey now," Burke said. He was pointing at something. Amos realized it was one of Julia's exposed breasts. He quickly pulled her bra and shirt back down over it.

Burke grinned. "She's not too bad on the eyes, is she? Takes care of herself. Getting a peek at a titty is always something to be grateful for, though I've always appreciated a nice ass more than anything. That's my kryptonite. You two ever ...?"

"No," Amos answered. He stood and turned around. "You're right about her needing medical attention. I have a proposition."

Burke ran a hand over his shaved scalp. "Yeah?"

"Release more hostages. That'll buy you more time."

"Time for what?"

"To keep speaking your mind to all those people out there."

Burke took out a cigarette and prepared to light it. "Shit, I don't know anymore."

"You can't smoke that in here. The entire school is a tobacco-free zone. There are signs posted outside."

Burke struck a match, took a long drag, and stared

at the gun-bulge in Amos's pants. "I saw those signs. They were right next to the gun-free zone ones. Funny how people choose to follow some rules and ignore others."

Julia groaned, opened her eyes, fell forward, and then vomited. Amos grabbed a towel, used it to gently wipe around her mouth, and then placed it over the runny brown puddle of coffee and vodka at her feet.

"I see that gun you're hiding in your pants," Burke said. "I'm also pretty sure I saw you pointing it at her head right before I came in. Maybe you forgot about this being a gun-free zone. Kind of like how I'm happy to forget there's no smoking allowed."

"I was holding the gun. I wasn't pointing it at her. She had just fallen down."

Burke looked at the floor. "That right? Where's all the blood? Head wound like that is sure to bleed quite a bit at first."

"I cleaned it up."

"Did you now? And when did you find the time to do that? You told me she had just fallen down."

"That's right."

Burke shook his head. "You're one slippery dude, I'll give you that."

"How so?"

"Because you lie, Mr. Diaz. I know your kind all too well. Been dealing with people like you most my life. You know all the words but hardly ever use them to speak the truth. I don't know what the hell you were doing with this poor woman in here, but I know it wasn't right. You're all kinds of fucked up. I can see it in your eyes. If a soul is a light, that light starting to go dark inside you a long time ago."

Amos grabbed the Glock and pointed it at Burke. "That's enough."

Burke stepped toward Amos and leaned forward until his forehead touched the tip of the barrel. "No more fancy words, Mr. Diaz. Put up or shut up. Pull that trigger or don't. Let's see what you're really made of. What's it gonna be?"

Before Amos could answer, Burke grabbed hold of his wrist and throat and threw him against the wall. The gun dropped to the floor. Burke kicked it away and then crashed an elbow into the side of Amos's jaw. When Amos attempted to free himself, Burke wrapped one arm under and around his neck while pushing his other arm against the back of his head so the oxygen to Amos's brain was instantly cut off. He managed all this with a cigarette still dangling from his lips.

"That's the thing about breathing," Burke said. "Nothing works without it. What you're feeling right now is a basic military choke hold. You promise to behave yourself and I'll let go. You keep thinking you can fight me, and it'll be lights out. Nod if you understand."

Amos gritted his teeth and nodded. Burke blew out a plume of tobacco smoke. "That's a good boy."

"Let him go." Both men looked up to find Julia pointing the Glock at them. "You heard me. Let him go and step away."

Burke released Amos and moved to the side. "Seems you made quite the recovery," he said. "Gotta admire a woman with that kind of grit."

When Amos started to walk toward her, Julia shook her head. "No, you stay right there."

"What do you mean?" Amos asked.

"I mean just what I said. Don't move until I tell you to."

"Why are you pointing the gun at me?"

Burke chuckled and then took another drag from his cigarette. "Jesus, she's not stupid. It wasn't more than two minutes ago you had that same gun pointed at her head."

"Put that out," Julia said.

"Huh?"

"The cigarette. Smoking isn't allowed on school grounds. Put it out."

Burke flicked the smoldering butt onto the floor and stomped it dead. "Man, they got you teachers so attached to rules, you have no sense of perspective. There's a hole in the back of your head, you're pointing a gun at two people, and the thing you need to deal with at this particular time is a goddamn smoke?"

Julia's eyes narrowed as she clenched her jaw. "I hate the smell."

Burke held up his hands. "You're holding the weapon. Guess that means you're in charge. So, what now?"

"You two are going out there and sitting down. Then we're all walking out of here together."

"Wait," Amos said. "That's not a good idea. It's too soon."

Julia looked at him like he'd just grown a second head. "Too soon for what?"

Burke used his thumb to point at Amos. "Too soon for whatever game he's been playing this whole time. He's had us all jumping on command. Ain't that right, Mr. Diaz?"

"I don't know what you're talking about."

"Oh, I think you do. In fact, I think you're actually enjoying all this."

"Nothing could be further from the truth."

Burke wagged a finger in Amos's face. "There you go again. Using those words to lie and keep your truth hidden. It took me a while but I'm on to you now."

"Hey," Julia said. "I'm the one you both need to be listening to. Open the door, go out there, and sit down."

Amos was rubbing his neck where Burke had squeezed it. "Julia, please consider what I have to say. If law enforcement sees you holding a weapon, they won't hesitate to shoot. There's a better way—my way."

"Fuck your way, Amos. Get moving."

Burke opened the door. "You heard the lady. Let's go." Burke went first. Julia walked behind Amos while keeping the gun pointed at his back.

Both Dardner and Randal got up. "What's going on?" Dardner asked.

Burke tipped his head toward Julia. "You'll have to ask her. She's in charge now."

"Everyone sit down," Julia said. "Wait, where is—"

The tip of Walter's rifle pressed against her lower back. "We'll take that," Walter said as Waylon came up on the other side of Julia, took the Glock from her, and placed it into his father's outstretched hand.

Burke smiled. "Well done, boys." He pointed to the chair he had just vacated. "Now, how about you have a seat there, Ms. Hodson? The same goes for the rest of you. Sit on down. She's right about one thing. We're gonna have ourselves a little talk."

Dardner gasped. "Julia, you're bleeding."

Julia sat down, patted the back of her head and then looked down at the blood on her fingers. "I'm fine."

"You most certainly are not," Dardner exclaimed. "You need medical attention." He stared at Burke. "Let her go."

Burke shrugged. "I intend to."

"You do?"

"Sure, just as soon as we finish hashing out a few things. That okay with you, Mr. Principal?"

"As long as you keep your promise to let her go."

Burke glanced at Amos. "I'm not the liar here."

A helicopter flew over the library's roof close enough it caused some books to fall from the shelves. Walter went to the door and then backed away slowly. "It's all smoky out there," he said.

"Stay put," Burke told the others as he went to the door to look for himself. "Seems they've dropped some tactical smoke bombs into the courtyard. Shit's about to get real." He turned toward Amos. "You said you had a plan to get us some more time?"

"That's right. Hopefully it's not too late. I need to make a call."

"Okay then," Burke said. "You make that call."

Amos took out his phone and then paused. "It involves letting some of us go."

"I figured as much. Go ahead."

Amos held the phone up to his face while the others listened. "Officer Markley, it's me. Yes, I'm fine. Mr. Burke is prepared to release some more hostages, but the authorities need to pull back from the school first. That's correct. Let me know what she says. I'll be waiting. Thank you."

Burke continued watching the courtyard. "You think that'll work?"

"I do," Amos answered. "Either way, we'll know soon enough."

Dardner cleared his throat. "Amos, what's going on? Are you actually working with Mr. Burke?"

"No, I'm just trying to keep everyone safe. Now shut up."

"Well," Burke said as he held up the Glock, "this is his so make of that what you will."

Dardner's head snapped sideways as he glared at Amos. "Is that really your weapon?"

"I thought I told you to shut up."

"I most certainly will not. Now answer my question."

Julia had been sitting quietly with her eyes closed. She opened them. "Yeah, it's his gun."

"How would you know that?" Dardner asked.

Julia winced as she touched the back of her head. "What difference does it make? It's here. Mr. Burke's holding it and I have no doubt he knows how to use it."

"But why would a teacher bring a gun to school? It's against the rules. This is a gun-free zone. Surely Mr. Diaz won't attempt to plead ignorance of the law."

Amos answered his phone. "Yes. That sounds fair. Thank you." He looked at Burke. "You get an additional hour for every hostage you release but you have to decide within the next five minutes or they're coming in."

Burke pointed to Julia. "You go first. They can get you to a doctor."

"No," Julia said. "I'm not leaving."

Amos turned to her. "What? Why not?"

"Because I want to be a part of what's going on here."

Dardner reached over and put his hand on Julia's knee. "He's letting you go, Ms. Hodson. Do as he says. That's an order."

Julia brushed the hand away. "An order? You don't have the power to be ordering anyone right now." She locked eyes with Burke. "I'm staying. Let Randal and your sons go. They're students. That'll look best to the public."

Amos nodded. "That's actually an excellent idea. Release the kids. It'll create an opportunity for your sons to get out of this without much blame. They can tell the authorities they were only doing what you told them to do."

Walter shook his head. "No fucking way. I'm not leaving you, Dad. We're in this together, remember?" He looked Randal up and down. "Besides, why should this piece of shit get to taste freedom before he's made to answer for what he's done?"

"And what exactly did he do?" Burke asked. "Waylon, could you be so kind as to help us out with that piece of the puzzle? Or I can just put my gun to his head and pull the trigger. Is that what you really want?"

Randal's face went white as his eyes filled with tears. "I didn't do nothing wrong. We were friends is all and then we weren't. That was it. I promise. That's how it was. I'm not lying."

"What do you think, Waylon? Is old Randal telling us the truth?"

Waylon shrugged while avoiding his father's gaze. "I don't know."

"What do you mean you don't know? What the hell have you done? What did you go and make your brother and me do? Look at me when I'm talking to you."

"See?" Randal's voice was both pleading and hopeful. "He made it all up. I didn't do anything to him."

"You calling my boy a liar?" Burke seethed.

"No," Randal whispered. "He was confused is all. I'm sure he didn't mean anything by it."

"The hell I didn't," Waylon said. "You ignored me. Even when I tried to ask what was wrong, you ignored me. All you wanted was to hang out with those stupid girls. I wanted to see you hurt. To hurt like you made me hurt. You can't treat people like you treated me. It's not right. I loved—"

Burke's mouth was a tight-lipped slash. "You loved what?"

"I loved him, and I thought he loved me, but I was wrong because he doesn't love nothing or nobody but himself."

"I knew it," Randal exclaimed. "I knew he was gay

for me. How he always wanted to hug and shit. It got weird. I told you I'm no fag."

Burke strode across the library until he stood looming over Randal. "That's the last word you'll ever say to me about that, understood?"

Randal nodded. Burke looked down at his feet, wiped his forehead with the back of his hand, and then let out a long sigh. "What the fuck do I do now?"

Amos got up. "You let them go, but you need to hurry. We don't have much time."

"Why not just let everyone go?" Burke said as he stared at Waylon. "This whole shitstorm was based on a lie that came out of your mouth. You told your brother how Randal touched you wrong. Said he was a pervert. Now, after all this, we finally learn the truth. What the hell is wrong with you, boy? Do you have any idea what you've done? You might as well have put the gun to my head and pulled the trigger yourself but seeing as you're nothing but a lying little coward, I suppose I'll have to go and do it."

Both Walter and Waylon cried out together. "No!"

The corners of Burke's mouth twitched as he pressed the Glock hard against his temple. "Fuck this shit. Try to do right and for what? Just to get stomped on by the last ones you would think to hurt you. Fuck it all. I'm done."

"Mr. Burke," Amos said. "Look at me. Let the boys go and then we'll have time to make something good from all this mess. I promise. I'm going to call Officer Markley and let him know they're coming out. Is that okay?"

"I won't go to prison," Burke replied. "I won't do it.

I won't do shit for anybody anymore."

Amos took out his phone. "I'm going to make the call now."

Burke shrugged. Amos contacted Markley and convinced him to give them three more hours for the three students who were being released. He told Walter and Waylon to leave their rifles with their father. When Waylon tried to say he was sorry, Burke turned his back on him and told him to get out and do what his older brother told him. The three boys left the library. A minute later, Markley called Amos to tell him they were safely in the parking lot being questioned by the FBI.

"We have three more hours, Mr. Burke," Amos said. "I suggest we use them."

Burke grunted. "Three hours? For what?"

Amos pursed his lips, cocked his head, and shrugged. "Let's find out, shall we?"

CHAPTER 20

2:34 p.m.

"I need a drink."

The others watched Amos turn around, go into the office, and then return with the bottle of vodka.

"What is that doing in there?" Dardner asked.

Amos unscrewed the cap, tipped the bottle back, and had a long drink. "This?" he said. "This is joining our group. Have a swig, you tight-ass."

Burke laughed as he struck a match and lit another cigarette. "Sometimes I almost like you, Diaz. You might just be as crazy as me."

"Please don't smoke in here." Dardner glared at Amos. "And no drinking. It's not allowed."

Amos handed Burke the bottle. Burke held his cigarette in one hand and the vodka in the other. "It's not allowed," he said in a high-pitched voice right before taking a drink and plopping the cigarette back into his mouth.

"My turn," Julia said. Dardner's face turned a dark red as he shook his head so hard it made his cheeks quiver. "Absolutely not, Ms. Hodson. Don't force my hand. I will file an incident report. It'll go on your permanent record."

Julia cradled the bottle on her lap and leaned forward. "You're pathetic, Dardner. I didn't really see that before, but I sure see it now. You ever just relax? Enjoy a moment? Not worry about the rules every stupid minute of every stupid day? Besides, my head is killing me. This will help."

Dardner stiffened in his seat. "I'm the principal of this school. I'm responsible for everything that happens here. I can't afford to ignore the rules. The rules are what keep us all safe. You disappoint me, Ms. Hodson."

"Rules don't keep people safe, you idiot," Burke grumbled. He blew smoke into Dardner's face, sat back in his chair, and stretched his legs out in front of him. "If rules kept us safe, why do we have so many problems? How many kids are gonna be killed in places like Chicago this week, huh? Aren't there rules against killing? Seems they don't do much. No, rules are made to help pussified losers like you feel safe, but down deep, you know different. The only thing keeping me from snapping your neck like a dry chicken bone right now is me. That's it. My choice. Not some rule."

Dardner folded his arms and sniffed. "Take away that gun and you're not so tough."

Burke's chin dropped toward his chest as he looked at Dardner from beneath heavy-lidded eyes. "Is that right?"

"Yes. You're just a bully, Mr. Burke, and I'm not afraid of you."

"This place probably has all kinds of rules against bullying, doesn't it?"

"Of course. Sky Valley High is proud to provide students a safe and respectful learning environment."

"Oh, is that what this is? Safe and respectful?"

"This," Dardner said, "is you violating that safety and respect. Your actions today represent the opposite of everything this school strives to be."

"What a crock. Principal must be another word for bullshit."

"And Burke must be another name for deranged lunatic."

Burke's cigarette smoldered where it dangled from the corner of his mouth. "I'm gonna smack you one. Just thought you should know before I go and do it."

"What? No—"

Burke got up. Dardner hid his face behind his hands. "Keep him away from me," he squeaked.

"Goddamn," Burke said with a shake of his head. "There's not an ounce of courage left in you, is there? You're just this puddle of nothing clinging to stupid rules while getting off talking down to others. Have a drink. Seems you need it more than any of us."

Dardner scowled. "I already told you. Drinking isn't allowed on campus."

Swop. That was the sound Burke's fist made when it struck Dardner's face. Burke sat back down like he didn't have a care in the world. Dardner spit out blood and tried not to cry while Amos and Julia shared a look that indicated neither of them were terribly bothered by the violence they had just seen delivered against their principal.

Burke blew out another swirling cloud of smoke.

"Stop fussing. You're fine. Have that drink. Call it peer pressure if it makes you feel any better. Or not. I could give a shit."

"You're a violent man, Mr. Burke," Dardner said.

"Yeah, but at least I'm a man which is a hell of a lot more than can be said for the likes of you. Go on and keep talking down to me, Mr. Principal. You haven't seen real violence yet. Not even close. There isn't a rule on this earth that'll keep you safe from a man like me. I could reach on over and kill you right now. Kill you quick. Kill you slow. Kill you however I want and there wouldn't be a damn thing you could do to stop it. I'd watch the life leave those watery eyes of yours and smile knowing the last thing you ever felt on this earth would be my hands around your scrawny neck. You really want to play in the dark with hell, Mr. Principal? I can bring it. Just say the fucking word."

"Are you two going to just sit there and let him threaten me?" Dardner whined to Amos and Julia.

"What are we supposed to do about it?" Julia asked.

"You could do something besides doing nothing."

"Really?" Amos said. "We're supposed to save you? You're the principal. Save yourself. Besides, this feels more than a little like karma coming back to bite you in the ass."

Dardner used his sleeve to wipe away the blood from under his nose. "Karma, Mr. Diaz? And what could you possibly mean by that?"

"I mean the guy who spends more time around here cooped up in his private office, who ignores young female students while they're being harassed not more than forty feet away from him, who calls in teachers, asks them some questions, and then writes down a few words taken out of context on their big yellow pad to be used against them later, isn't really in a position to think those same teachers are now going to go out of their way to save him from the big bad man who wants to punch him in the mouth for being disrespectful."

"Ah, now I see. It's personal."

"Personal? Sure, maybe it is. I've never made it a secret I don't like you much."

"For God's sake, Mr. Diaz, we're talking about a man with a gun. Are you really so unwilling to put aside workplace differences in the face of such a threat?"

"He just gave you a little smack. It's not like he put a bullet into your skull. Why not just save yourself and have a drink like he's asking?"

Dardner's brows lifted. "My goodness, you really are working with this maniac, aren't you?"

"Sure."

"See? You're not even denying it. Sooner or later, the authorities will come through those doors. I look forward to giving the FBI my statement about your complicity."

"I have no doubt you are. In the meantime, we have more than a couple hours left. Why not try to enjoy it? Have a drink and then we'll all have a nice chat."

"You and your chat can go to hell."

Burke grabbed Dardner's throat. "That's not polite. He's actually trying to keep you from getting your face caved in. You should be thanking him. Either you take a drink or I'm gonna get seriously upset. Put that head back and say ah. Go on. Do it."

Dardner closed his eyes, moved his head back, and opened his mouth. Julia handed the bottle to Burke and then watched as Burke poured vodka down Dardner's throat until he started to cough it back up.

"Yeah," Burke said grinning. "That's more like it. See? Now you're one of us."

Dardner looked like he was about to burst into tears. "You people are insane."

Amos clicked his tongue. "You people? Did you really just say that? There are a lot of things I don't like about you, Principal Dardner, but I never took you for a racist."

"I am no racist. How dare you."

Amos rolled his eyes. "Geez you're easy to wind up. I'm ready to talk. Are you?"

"I have nothing to say to any of you. I'll just sit here and wait for the authorities and then watch them haul you away."

Amos got up. "That actually gives me an idea." He looked at Burke. "You mind if I turn on the news?"

Burke lit another cigarette. "I don't give a shit."

"I just need to go grab the remote. It's in the office."

"Sure, whatever."

When Amos came back, he turned on the television mounted over the counter that separated the office and the main part of the library. A female reporter stood next to a large crowd of people and then instructed her cameraman to show a smaller group of protesters who were lined up in front of the school's main entrance.

"Will you look at that," Burke murmured. "Those people are all holding rifles."

Dardner shook his head. "What a damn circus. This is horrible."

Julia pointed at the screen. "Look there." It was a man holding a sign that said, We stand with Willy Burke.

Amos glanced at Burke. "See? What you said matters. People heard it. You're not alone."

"Where are my boys?" Burke asked.

"Most likely still with the authorities," Amos replied. "They'll be fine."

"He's lying to you," Dardner said. "Your sons will be sent to juvenile detention. Walter is most likely to be tried as an adult. He's looking at a very long jail sentence."

Amos passed Burke the bottle. "Don't listen to him."

Burke took a sip while his eyes remained locked onto the television. "Turn it up," he said. The same female reporter was interviewing a stern-faced, middle-aged woman who had a hunting rifle slung over her shoulder. She stared into the camera and spoke her mind.

"I'm not saying what Willy Burke did this morning at the school is right, but I know why he did it. The whole system is a mess, and we're sick and tired of it. These schools are a cancer. They don't teach kids anymore. They just try to indoctrinate them. The schools, the government, they keep pushing and pushing and taking and taking and eventually, somebody is going to want to push back and take back, and that's what he's trying to do. And I don't think he's just doing it for himself. He's doing it for all of us."

The reporter leaned in closer to the woman. "Are you saying you support the man who showed up to this school with weapons and took people hostage?"

"No, I said that part of what he did wasn't right. Don't try and put words in my mouth that aren't mine. You news people do that kind of thing way too much. What I mean is, Willy Burke is a man fed up with how things in this country are, and a lot of that mess starts with the schools. They don't teach reading and writing anymore. It's all about social justice and gender identity and a bunch of other nonsense. I have a granddaughter in another school, and you want to know something? Her teacher can hardly speak a word of English. That's right. I swear to God she comes home and says she can't understand what the teacher is teaching. The handful of Mexican kids can, but the rest of them are playing catch-up. My tax dollars are going toward a school that isn't doing right by my granddaughter."

"So, you're anti-immigration?"

"What? No. Again, that's not what I said. Look, if a teacher in this country is teaching a class that is mostly English-speaking students, is it wrong to think that teacher should know how to speak American?"

The reporter smirked. "You mean speak English?"

"Yeah, you know what I meant. How about you take that microphone and shove it in someone else's face? You and I are done. Bye-bye."

The reporter faced the camera, informed viewers there had been as many as seventeen arrests of protesters at the school already, and that it appeared more were likely to follow. Dardner rubbed his temples.

"Ignorance layered upon more ignorance. To know women like her breed more of her kind should frighten all of us."

"Excuse me?" Julia said. "How can you possibly think you're so superior? That woman is a mother and a grandmother. Everyone deserves to be respected, Doyle. And frankly, she has a valid complaint. I have a nephew in middle school in another state. Every assignment he gets is written both in English and Spanish. He's in sixth grade. I'm all for immigration. I love everybody, but anyone who lives in this country should learn to speak English or the whole system is going to break down into these separate tribes that are constantly at war with each other. We have to stop putting labels on everyone and everything. When I was a kid, we all grew up knowing we were American and what that meant. Despite individual differences, we all shared that common foundation. Now? These kids today don't seem to know anything about who they are. They're just angry and confused and willing to latch onto just about anything that feeds their need to feel important. That's not healthy, it's not sustainable, and sooner or later, we're all going to be paying the price."

Amos clapped his hands together. "Yes. That's exactly the kind of conversation I'm talking about."

Burke smiled at Julia. "I didn't understand everything you said, but it sure sounded good and I'm pretty sure I agree with most of it."

Julia smiled back. "Thanks."

"I have an idea," Amos said, "but I need everyone to agree." He looked at Dardner. "Well, maybe not everyone."

Burke had another sip of vodka. "Go ahead. Tell us what you're thinking."

"I make a call to one of the local news stations, put the phone down between us all, and we transmit the conversation to the outside world. It's just another version of the intercom but we all get to talk and everyone else is able to listen."

Dardner pursed his lips. "Mr. Diaz, why are you so willing to provide the man who took the students and staff of this school hostage a platform to speak his mind?"

"Because his story deserves to be heard as much as anyone else's. And, because the things we were just talking about, how we as a society educate ourselves—how we interact, communicate, hope, and dream—these are subjects that are not discussed honestly anymore. Julia is absolutely right. Our current culture pushes people into corners. All this technology that promised to bring us together is actually tearing us apart. We've forgotten how to honestly interact on the most basic, human level."

Dardner crossed his legs and tilted his head. "And what does any of that possibly have to do with Mr. Burke's reprehensible actions today? Need I remind you he is still keeping us here in this room via the threat of further violence?"

Amos nodded. "Yes, what he did was wrong, but his reasons might be right. If you don't want to participate, that's fine. Just sit there and be quiet. The choice is yours."

"Oh? Really? Then I choose to get up and walk out."

"No. You stay. When we leave, we'll leave together."

"Then, Mr. Diaz, I vote that we leave now."

"It's not yet time."

"So, both you and Mr. Burke are the ones keeping me hostage? I'll be sure to remember that when I speak to the authorities."

"You do whatever you want."

"Oh, I intend to. Believe me."

Julia stood. "Wait. I want to get something from the office."

"What?" Amos asked.

"It's a surprise. Besides, I'm not positive it's still there."

"Go ahead," Burke said. Amos shrugged. Julia disappeared into the office and then returned with one hand behind her back. All three men leaned forward as they waited to see what she was hiding.

Julia stood with her feet shoulder-width apart and held up a joint.

Amos's eyes widened. "Is that ..."

"Oh yeah."

Burke's grin widened until his face looked like it might crack open. "God bless you. Girl, I knew you were one of the good ones."

Dardner sat back in his chair. "Mr. Diaz comes back with alcohol and you come back with drugs. My, what a disappointingly irresponsible staff I have working at this school. That is marijuana in your hand, correct?"

"Yes," Julia said without hesitation. "And it's good stuff."

Dardner waved his hands in front of him. "No-no-no, cigarettes, alcohol, and now this? Absolutely not. This is beyond the pale."

Burke took the joint from Julia and lit it up. The library was soon filled with the pungent, heavy-sweet-burning scent of high-quality weed. Burke, Julia, and Amos all had deep hits. Amos offered the joint to Dardner who quickly refused.

"Fine," Julia said. "More for the rest of us."

It took them nearly thirty minutes to finish the joint. Burke sighed. "You're right," he said. "That was some good shit."

Amos took out his phone. "Are we ready to talk?" Julia and Burke nodded.

"Okay, let me look up the news station's number and then I'll make the call."

The woman who answered connected Amos to the news director who immediately agreed. Amos carefully set the phone down on the floor in the middle of the group, held up three fingers, and then silently counted down to zero.

The conversation began.

CHAPTER 21

3:13 p.m.

"My name is Amos Diaz. I'm a history teacher at Sky Valley High. With me now is art teacher, Julia Hodson, and school principal, Doyle Dardner. The man who has generously allowed us to speak with all of you is Willy Burke. Mr. Burke, would you like to start us off?"

Burke kept quiet as he stared at the floor. Amos cleared his throat. "Uh, okay, I guess I'll be the one to begin. As most of you out there likely know already, Mr. Burke allowed everyone who was in the courtyard to go free. I would like to personally thank him for that decision."

"As would I," Julia said.

"I appreciate that," Burke replied. "I didn't come here today to see anyone get hurt. I know that's gonna be hard for some of you to understand, but it's the truth. I just wanted a chance to speak and be heard. Seems that's been pretty much impossible for me and a lot of others in this country for far too long."

Dardner shook his head. "That's simply not true, Mr. Burke. We all know what you are by your actions today."

"Yeah?" Burke replied. "So, go on and tell me. What am I?"

"A domestic terrorist. A bully. A thug. And most certainly a dangerous criminal."

Burke gave Dardner a thin smile, but his eyes were ice. "Well, fuck you too."

Amos held up his hands and leaned forward in the chair. "As everyone can hear, opinions are running strong in our little group, and that's okay. That's what America is supposed to be all about—a free and open exchange of ideas."

"Oh please." Dardner spoke through partly clenched teeth. "We're here because Mr. Burke has a gun and he won't let us leave. That's it. I would also add that this gun belongs to you, Mr. Diaz. Perhaps you'd care to explain that to the authorities who I'm sure are listening."

"Sure, it's my handgun. I carry it for protection. You bring up a pertinent subject, Principal Dardner: school safety. Please explain why it is that the school district's resource officer, Officer Markley, is not allowed to carry a weapon while on the job?"

"Officer Markley is unarmed because that is district policy as voted on by the school board."

Amos turned to Burke. "Mr. Burke, would you have still come to the school today if you knew it had armed security on campus?"

"No," Burke said. "My plan didn't include anyone getting hurt. Armed security officers would have meant a shootout. That means injuries or worse, and that's the last thing I wanted to see happen. I really don't care if Mr. Principal believes me or not. I came here today to speak my mind and to do right by my boys. That's it."

Dardner appeared ready to bolt from his chair. "That's a lie, Mr. Burke, and you know it. If you were truly concerned for people's safety, you never would have taken the school hostage in the first place."

Burke locked eyes with Dardner for several long seconds. "If I wanted you dead, you'd be dead."

"Well, you did assault me."

"What? A couple love taps? Shit, that ain't assault. Not where I come from."

"Clearly, you and I come from very different places then. Now how about we get back to the fact Mr. Diaz brought a gun to school, which is a direct violation of district and state policy and the reason we are now being held hostage."

Burke put the gun on his lap. "I brought my own gun. I didn't need this one. Speaking of which, where's my revolver?"

"I hid it," Amos said.

Burke grunted. "That right? Then I guess it's only fair I took yours."

Dardner pointed to the rifles at Burke's feet. "What about those? You didn't come to this school merely to speak words, Mr. Burke. You came here to terrify, threaten, and intimidate."

Burke picked up the assault rifle. "You want this? Go ahead. Take it."

Julia glanced at Amos who then mouthed the words it's okay to her.

"Go on," Burke persisted. "Take the damn thing if

it worries you so much."

"You're bluffing," Dardner said. "You have no intention of giving that weapon to me."

"Take the gun, you squirmy little maggot."

Burke placed the rifle next to Dardner's chair. Dardner looked at Amos. "It's a trap. He'll shoot me before I pick it up."

"No, he won't," Julia replied. "Isn't that right, Mr. Burke? You promise?"

The ice in Burke's eyes melted some when he smiled at Julia. "Yeah, I promise. He's good to go."

Dardner reached down slowly. One hand closed around the rifle and then the other. He brought it toward him, gripped it tight, and then pointed it at Burke.

"You want me to shoot you? Is that it?"

Burke stood, stuck the Glock into the front of his pants, and folded his arms across his chest. "You don't have the stones to pull that trigger."

"I wouldn't be so sure of that, Mr. Burke."

Julia put her hand on Amos's arm. "Do something," she whispered.

Burke arched a brow. "Yeah?" he said to Dardner. "Prove it."

Dardner glanced down at the phone. "Let the record show I do not wish to harm Mr. Burke, but I will defend myself if need be."

Burke frowned. "Who the hell are you talking to? I'm the one right in front of you. You talk to me."

"Please sit back down, Mr. Burke. I don't want to hurt you."

"How about for once in your miserable life you

stand up, Mr. Principal? Let's see what you got. Instead of killing all these school kids slowly like you've been doing, you have your chance to kill me quickly right here and now."

"I don't wish to kill anyone."

"Hmmm, know what? I think you do. I think you'd like nothing more than to be given a chance to hand down a death sentence. Principal, prison warden—it's all pretty much the same thing."

"I'm sorry you see it that way."

"On your feet."

"Why? Do you plan to hurt me if I get up?"

"No, I'm trying to help you."

The look Dardner gave Burke made it clear he thought he couldn't be trusted. "You help me? After all that you've done today, I find that very hard to believe."

"Take it or leave it. Last chance."

Dardner got up holding the gun firmly in his hands. Burke winked at him. "See? That wasn't so hard. Now you're the one with all the power. The question now is what are you gonna do with it?"

"Honestly, I'm not sure."

"Yeah," Burke said with a nod. "It's not so easy, is it?"

"What's that?"

"Pulling the trigger. Killing is the simple part. It's the forgetting. Man, that's where it really gets you and drags you down bit by bit until there's nothing of yourself left."

Dardner took a deep breath as he lifted the rifle until it pointed at Burke's neck. "We're walking out of here now, Mr. Burke."

"Are you?"

"Yes."

"You'll have to pull that trigger first. Make yourself worthy of the freedom you want. Be a man, Mr. Principal. You know what a man is?"

"I believe I have the general idea."

"Prove it. Fire away."

Julia's eyes darted from Burke to Dardner. "C'mon you two, stop it."

"I'm in charge now, Ms. Dodson," Dardner said. "You and Mr. Diaz will be coming with me."

Amos looked at Julia and shook his head. They both remained seated.

Dardner spoke more loudly. "I said you can get up. I wasn't asking. It's time to go. That's an order."

"You giving orders now, Mr. Principal?" Burke looked like he was trying not to laugh.

"Something funny?" Dardner asked.

"No sir. You're the boss. How long do we have to wait to find out if you really have what it takes?"

"Dardner's jaw clenched. "Stay put. Don't do anything stupid."

Burke jutted his chin out and stepped toward Dardner until the tip of the rifle pressed against his neck. "So far you're all talk. Let's see what you got. C'mon now. We're all waiting. All of us here and everyone out there listening. Grow a goddamn pair and do it."

The blood drained from Dardner's face. "What's wrong with you?"

"I'm right as rain, Mr. Principal. At this rate, I'm

gonna die of old age before you find the courage to be a man, a real man. Not the phony version that passes for one in places like this."

"Killing someone doesn't make you a man."

Burke grabbed hold of the rifle barrel. "What do you know about it?"

"Are you referring to manhood or killing?"

Burke's barking laugh crashed against the library's concrete walls. "Shit, I'm pretty sure you're ignorant of both. Tell you what. You have three seconds before I rip this weapon away and beat you with it."

Dardner's eyes blinked rapidly. "What?"

"Yeah, here we go. Now it gets real. You ready? I'm starting the countdown."

There was a pause. Dardner shook his head slowly from one side to the other. "Please, don't do it."

"Three," Burke said.

"I won't shoot you."

"Two."

"For God's sake, Mr. Burke," Dardner pleaded. "Stop it."

Burke pressed the rifle even harder against his neck so that it made his voice a raspy croak. "One."

Dardner pulled the trigger.

Julia screamed.

A helicopter thundered directly over the school.

And Amos grinned.

CHAPTER 22

3:37 p.m.

Burke didn't die. It wasn't even close, but he was impressed by Dardner's willingness to try and make that death happen.

"Man, you really did it. Didn't think you had it in you."

Dardner pulled the trigger again and again. Burke shrugged.

"It isn't loaded—never was. Same as the hunting rifle."

"You mean to tell me you and your sons showed up to the school with weapons that weren't loaded? But I heard gunfire."

"Oh, that. Yeah, that was me with the pistol—the one Mr. Diaz has hidden somewhere in here. It's not really loaded either."

"What the hell are you talking about? I just told you I heard the shots."

Both Julia and Amos stared at Burke waiting to hear his explanation.

"Blanks," Burke said.

Dardner's eyes narrowed. "Blanks? Bullshit."

"It's true. If Mr. Diaz wants to go grab my gun, I'll prove it."

Julia tugged on Amos's sleeve as she tilted her head toward the office. "Go get it," she whispered.

Dardner nodded. "Yes, Mr. Diaz, go retrieve Mr. Burke's weapon."

"Hold on," Amos replied. "He already has one gun. Now you want me to give him another?"

"You think I'm lying?' Burke asked.

Amos put his hands on his hips. "Are you saying you're not? Why would you attempt to take a school hostage with guns that weren't actually loaded with real bullets? These rifles are one thing. You didn't want your sons to potentially harm someone with them. But your own weapon? Why leave yourself so defenseless?"

"That's simple. Because I could, and I did. Places like this don't fight back. They're open targets. That's partly why I did it. To prove a point."

"And what point is that?" Dardner huffed.

"That the people running these schools, the ones whose job it is to keep kids safe, don't have a damn clue on how to do it. In fact, I'm not sure they even want to know. There's an entire industry built up around this school violence shit. It's all talk, and then they spend money on more talk, but nothing really gets done. Nothing changes. And the people, the teachers, the kids—they're just taught to lay down and die when someone rolls in to do them harm. Wait for the cops. Pray their lives are spared. Hope for the best. The entire country has turned into one big fucking slaughterhouse in waiting."

Dardner glanced at the rifle in his hands. "Are you suggesting we need more guns and not fewer in this country? That having more of what is killing us is somehow going to make us all safer?"

"If that rifle had fired, would you even need to be asking me that question? No, you wouldn't. I'd be dead, you'd be free, and the school would be safe. You see, that's how the real world works. It's a violent, fucked-up mess. You either plan and prepare, or sooner or later, it'll take you out."

"That's quite a civics lesson, Mr. Burke," Amos said.

"Don't know nothing about no civics, but I know plenty about living and dying—likely more than most and sure as hell more than any of you."

Julia pointed at the phone that was still on the floor transmitting their words to the world. Amos nodded. "Good, let them hear this. It's the kind of conversation this country should have been having with itself all along."

"Now about my gun..." Burke's voice trailed off.

"I'll get it," Amos answered. "But before I do, I want to make absolutely certain the others are in agreement."

Julia said she was fine with getting the other gun. Dardner wasn't. "How can we trust it's not a trick?" he said.

"Trick?" Amos scowled. "Why would Mr. Burke let me go into the office and come back out with a loaded weapon that could be used against him? That doesn't make any sense."

Dardner stared at Amos. "It does if you two really

are working together."

"That's as absurd now as it was when you first suggested it. Mr. Burke, did I have any prior knowledge of your actions today?"

"Nah," Burke answered. "This was all my doing. You having a gun on you, well, that was a bit of a surprise. I never thought to think a teacher might take the initiative to defend themselves. You're all such a violence-avoiding group of do-nothings."

Dardner grunted. "As if that's a bad thing."

"Didn't say it was," Burke replied. "Didn't say it wasn't. Just stating reality. Teachers these days seem to only fight for free food in the teachers' lounge and more money in their pockets."

Amos chuckled. "He's right about the food in the teachers' lounge. No denying that."

"I'm happy you find this all so amusing, Mr. Diaz."

"Is that some heavy sarcasm from you, Principal Dardner?"

"Yes, it is."

"Can I go get the gun?"

Dardner sighed. "Sure. Why not? At this point, what difference does it make?"

Amos went into the office and came back out aiming the pistol at Burke. "Is this really what you had in mind, Mr. Burke?"

"Sure. Go ahead. Fire away."

Julia and Dardner stepped back. Amos pointed the gun at the ceiling. "Everyone ready?"

Dardner nodded. "Go ahead."

Amos fired. The ceiling was left undamaged.

"See?" Burke said. "Blanks. Nobody at the school

was ever in any real danger. At least not from me."

Dardner turned to Amos. "Which also means the only armed threat came from you, Mr. Diaz. It's your weapon that is now in Mr. Burke's hand. It's your violation of school policy that remains the real threat. This is insane. All of it. I'm going outside and returning with the authorities, and all of you are going to be arrested."

Amos grabbed hold of Dardner's arm. "Sit down. This isn't done."

"Get your hand off me. Would you like me to add assault to the considerable trouble you're already in?"

"I'd listen to him if I were you, Mr. Principal," Burke said. "He's trying to keep you from getting hurt."

"Really? Are you going to shoot me in the back, Mr. Burke?"

"I'd rather not, but I will if I have to. Do like Mr. Diaz says and take a seat."

"No. I won't. I've had more than enough of this nonsense. I'm walking out of here right now and there's not a damn thing any of you are going to do about it."

Burke tilted his head toward the phone on the floor. "You playing it up? Is that it? You want them to think you're some brave hero or something?"

"I don't care what you think. This thing, whatever it is—the alcohol, the drugs, the guns—it's finished. I'm done. You're done. We're all done. There's nothing more to be gained from any of this. All that's happening is we're giving a platform to a disturbed man who needs help. I intend to walk out of here and start the process of getting him that help. Is that understood? Now get out of my way."

"Gee," Burke said, "you talk like I'm not even here."

"I'm leaving." Dardner yanked his arm away from Amos and took another step toward the exit.

"Hey, Doyle, is it true books aren't the only thing you've checked out of this library?"

Dardner whirled around. His cheeks burned red, but he said nothing. Julia's brows lifted.

"Well?"

"I don't know what you're talking about. Nor do I want to know. Drop it."

Burke scratched his beard with the tip of the Glock. "Your face says different, Mr. Principal. You look like you've seen a ghost or a little reminder that you did something you shouldn't have."

Dardner's eyes darted toward the phone. "Turn it off," he whispered.

Amos reached down and picked it up. "What? This? Why? Is there something you don't want anyone to hear?"

"Turn it off and I'll stay."

Amos ended the open call and slid the phone into the inside pocket of his jacket. "There. Have a seat."

Dardner plopped into the chair behind him and glowered at Julia.

"Don't you dare look at me like that," she said to him. When Dardner looked away she nodded. "That's better."

"Now I'm truly intrigued," Amos remarked as he sat.

"Yeah, what he said," Burke added. "What's the

pretty lady got on you, Mr. Principal?"

Dardner stiffened as he lifted his head. "That's not anyone's business. I'm still here. That's what you wanted, isn't it? So, get on with whatever this is so we can all go home."

Julia licked her lips. "I'm hungry. How about we order pizza?"

Burke threw his head back and howled laughter. "My God, girl, you really are one of a kind. There's always time for pizza. Am I right?"

"Now that you mention it," Amos said, "I'm getting hungry as well. I could go for a slice or two."

"Well, of course you're all hungry." Dardner spit out each word like it was something that tasted foul. "You're stoned. It's pathetic."

Julia leaned forward and stuck her lower lip out. "Oh, poor baby. It's pathetic."

This caused Burke to start laughing again as Dardner gritted his teeth. "I'm so happy I'm here to amuse you all."

Amos took out his phone and began to text Markley but then stopped. "What kind of toppings do we want?"

Burke went from laughing to serious in about a half-second. "Hmmm, I like sausage and olives but no onions. Those things upset my stomach. I'll be cramping for hours."

Julia's shoulders slumped. "Oh, I really love onions."

"Goddammit," Dardner shouted. "Just order a half and half and then shut up about it."

Burke snapped his fingers. "Yeah, half with onions

and half without. Good idea, Mr. Principal."

"So," Amos said. "Half with sausage and olives and half with sausage, olives, and onions?"

Julia scrunched her face together. "No, let's do Canadian bacon on one side and sausage on the other. That way it'll be easier to tell the difference."

"So, which has the onions, the sausage or the bacon?"

Julia looked at Amos and shrugged. "I don't care."

"Okay, we'll go with sausage and olives and Canadian bacon and onions. Everyone good with that?"

Even Dardner nodded his approval. Amos sent the text and waited. Markley called thirty seconds later. "You want us to deliver you a goddamn pizza? Is this some kind of sick joke, Mr. Diaz?"

"We're hungry," Amos answered.

"Then walk out of there with your hands up so we can all go home. You're hungry? Yeah, me too. We're all hungry."

"Let us eat, we'll talk a little more, and then I think this will all be wrapped up soon. I promise."

"Wrapped up? What do mean by that?"

"I mean it'll be what everyone wants. Nobody is hurt, and we go free."

"Huh," Markley said. "Not likely. Burke is going to jail."

"You know what I mean."

"No, I don't. Is everyone still okay in there?"

"We're fine. You heard us talking to each other, right?"

"Yes, Mr. Diaz, we heard you talking. The news

agencies out here are loving it. At least while you're talking, the protestors quiet down."

"Then I guess we should get back to talking."

"Wait, the pizza, where do you want us to leave it?"

"In the courtyard. Just put the box on the ground. I'll come out and grab it. Make sure all the cops stay back. Mr. Burke has my word there won't be any trouble—just food."

"Is he still armed?"

"Yes."

"With your gun?"

"Correct."

"You know you're going to have to answer some tough questions about that."

Amos nodded while holding the phone against his ear. "I know."

"Okay, we should have the pizza there pretty quickly. I'll text you when we're about to deliver it."

"Thank you, Officer Markley."

"Stay safe, Mr. Diaz."

Amos looked up and took a deep breath. "The pizza is on its way." He held up the phone. "Until then, should we keep talking?"

Burke and Julia nodded.

Dardner put his face into his hands and groaned.

The conversation continued.

CHAPTER 23

3:55 p.m.

"**Y**ou sure there are plates in here?" Amos asked.

"Yeah, I've had lunch with Ronda more times than I can remember," Julia answered. "Look in the cupboard right above the sink."

Amos found the plates and set them on the counter. He looked out into the library where Burke stood holding the Glock and stared at Dardner who sat with his arms crossed and his eyes closed. "The marijuana seems to have taken the edge off Mr. Burke. That was a good idea."

"Took the edge off me as well, but now I'm starving. I think I could eat the pages out of a phone book." Julia lowered her voice. "Do you think we're really getting out of here okay?"

"Yeah, I do. Burke's a troubled man, but he's no killer. If he was, he wouldn't have come to the school with weapons that weren't even loaded."

"He has your gun, Amos."

"I know."

"How much trouble are you in because of it?"

"Not sure."

"Are you going to lose your job?"

Amos shrugged. "Maybe. Probably."

"Do you care?"

"Honestly? No. Not really. I've been a ghost around here for some time. Why not make it official?"

"You don't really mean that. You're a teacher. What else would you do?"

"I don't know. Perhaps start living for the first time in a long time. That would be nice."

Julia massaged her neck and cleared her throat. "Does it still hurt?" Amos asked. "Your neck?"

"Yeah, a little."

"How about the back of your head?"

"That's more of a dull throb. I'm sure it'll feel a lot worse by tomorrow. I'm still running on adrenalin right now." Julia looked at the broken pencil sharpener. "We were fighting when I fell?"

"Yes. You were grabbing for my phone and slipped backwards."

"Slipped or pushed?"

"Does it matter? You're okay now and for that, I'm very grateful."

Julia stared at Amos long and hard and then nodded. "I suppose what is done is done, but now what? The weed is wearing off. Burke could go back to being agitated again."

"I know. That's why we'll keep him talking and we'll talk with him. He's a lonely, frustrated man who's desperate to vent that frustration with others he thinks are sympathetic to the things he's feeling."

"Are you?"

"Am I what?"

"Sympathetic to what Mr. Burke is saying."

"I suppose on some level, I am. He might be crazy, but that's doesn't mean he's entirely wrong."

"You're playing with fire, Amos."

"No, I'm trying to prevent us all from getting burned. He's almost ready to let us go. I know it."

"I hope you're right. We should get back in there before he gets suspicious and takes it out on Dardner."

"Speaking of Dardner, what did you mean when you said books aren't the only thing he's checked out of this library?"

"Oh, that. Well, let's just say our beloved principal isn't the great moral authority at this school that he would like us all to believe."

Amos arched a brow. "Ronda and him?"

"I don't want to say any more than I already have. Ronda asked that I not tell anyone, and I'd like to keep that promise."

"Huh. I had no idea. Dardner's been married for what, twenty years?"

"Something like that, yeah. He broke it off with Ronda last year and ever since, she says he's not exactly been pushing the district to maintain funding for the library."

"Why doesn't she report him? I have to believe the school board wouldn't take kindly to an administrator having relations with someone working beneath him—no pun intended."

"That kind of thing isn't strictly against district policy. And besides, Ronda has never been someone who starts trouble. She actually told me she loved him."

"Dardner? You've got to be kidding."

"I wish I was, but I'm not. She also said the sex was great."

Amos winced. "Ewww, too much information."

"You're right. I've already said way too much. Do me a favor and forget I told you anything."

"It's not easy to forget something like that. I always knew Dardner was a son-of-a-bitch. Now I get to add cheater to the list of reasons I don't like him."

Julia picked up the plates and moved toward the door. "We better get back out there before Burke thinks we're up to something."

Dardner looked up when Amos and Julia sat next to him. "That took a while," he said.

"It took what it took," Amos replied. "So, Mr. Burke, should I call the news station back, so we can pick up where we left off?"

"I prefer the intercom," Burke answered. "I like being able to hear the conversation while it's happening."

"You want me to bring the phone out here?"

"Is that a problem?"

"Not if the cord is long enough. I'll have to see."

After Amos went back to the office, Julia caught Burke staring at her. "What?"

Burke shook his head. "Nothing. Sorry, I didn't mean to make you uncomfortable."

"You're not. I was just wondering what you were looking at. I thought I might have a booger sticking out of my nose or something."

"No, nothing like that. It was just, oh, never mind."

"Tell me."

Burke took a deep breath. "It's just that I really wish you and me could have met under different, uh, circumstances."

"And why's that?"

"You seem like a nice woman. The kind I'd like to get to know better."

Julia didn't respond right away. The longer the silence went, the more Burke fidgeted in his chair. "Shit, I'm sorry. Now I really am making you uncomfortable. Forget it."

"I think you're interesting too, Mr. Burke," Julia said. "You never know. Maybe after all the dust settles from this day, we just might become friends."

Burke frowned. "Friends? At my age, I don't need any more friends."

Dardner opened his eyes. "Will you two please shut up? If you wish to flirt with a psychopath, Ms. Hodson, I would appreciate it if you did it on your own time and far removed from me."

"That's not nice." Burke leveled his gaze onto Dardner. "Tell the lady you're sorry."

"For what?"

Burke's movement out of his chair was both powerful and swift, like a predator launching itself from a just-opened cage. He grabbed hold of Dardner by the shirt and yanked him forward. "For being a prick. Now apologize."

Dardner put his hand around Burke's wrist and attempted to push his hand away. "Let me go."

"Apologize and I will."

"I didn't do anything to apologize for, you halfwit."

Burke tightened his grip on Dardner's shirt and then twisted the fabric until Dardner started to choke. "I don't care about you being an asshole to me, but you will apologize to her."

"That's okay," Julia said as she placed her hand on Burke's shoulder. "I'm fine. Really. There's no need for anyone to get hurt on my account."

Burke let go. Dardner sputtered, gasped, and then pointed at Julia. "The lovesick puppy listens to you. That's good. Why not tell him to let us all leave?"

"Stop talking like I'm not even here," Burke snarled right before smacking the side of Dardner's face with the back of his hand. "You felt that, right? See? I am here so start showing me some goddamn respect."

Dardner got up. His mouth was bleeding again.

"What's going on?" Amos asked while standing behind everyone with the phone in his hands.

"I'm waiting for Principal No-Dick to apologize," Burke answered.

Dardner dabbed his mouth with his fingers and then looked down at the blood. "It's time to pick sides, Mr. Diaz. Him or me. Choose now."

"Why would he choose you?" Julia yelled. "You've already threatened to tell the authorities about his gun. You've threatened me about the alcohol and drugs. Why would either one of us choose to help you?"

"Because we live in a society governed by rules, Ms. Hodson. You're a teacher. I would expect you of all people to understand that. Without those rules, there is anarchy in which beasts like Mr. Burke are allowed to run free and do as they please at the expense of everyone else around them. I choose not to live in such a world, and I thought you would feel the same. Apparently, I was mistaken. I assure you I won't make that mistake again."

"You whiney little bitch." Burke's lips drew back from his teeth giving him the appearance of a wolf ready to tear into its next meal. "I warned you to stop talking about me like I'm not here."

Amos set the phone down on a chair and then stepped between Burke and Dardner. "Just relax," he said.

Burke pushed against Amos's chest. "Get out of my way. He needs to be taught a lesson."

"You're probably right about that, but I can't let you hurt him. That does none of us any good. This day will come to an end, Mr. Burke. You must remember that and think about your sons. They need their father."

Amos's head rocked back as Burke pressed the Glock under his chin. "Get out of my way."

"No. You want to kill me with my own gun? Fine— go ahead."

"Please, Mr. Burke," Julia pleaded. "Don't do it."

Burke's eyes softened. He turned his head and looked down at Julia. "Call me Willy."

"Willy, I know you don't really want to hurt Amos. That's not who you are."

"That's exactly who he is," Dardner scoffed. "Violence is the only thing a man like him knows. It oozes out of every pore and dominates every stupid thought his mind can manage to form. He represents everything that is wrong in our society, including the wrong he has done to his own children. He's a thing to be punished, not made friends with."

"You know," Amos said. "I'd really appreciate it if you would stop pissing off the guy who has a gun to my face."

"What? Now you're afraid of him, Mr. Diaz? You were the one who invited him here. You were the one who armed him. You were the one who wanted to give him the opportunity to express himself. Well, mission accomplished. He's revealing his true colors to you. Congratulations. Now deal with the consequences."

Julia still had her hand on Burke's shoulder. "Don't listen to him, Willy. He's an asshole. Please put the gun down so we can keep talking. I want to hear what you have to say."

"Go ahead, Mr. Burke," Dardner said. "Embrace who you really are and pull that trigger."

Amos's eyes widened. Burke lowered the Glock and looked Dardner up and down. "You really are an asshole. Why would you want me to hurt one of your own teachers? What the fuck is wrong with you, man?"

When Burked stepped back, Amos whirled around and stood face-to-face with Dardner. "You son-of-a-bitch, you told him to shoot me."

Dardner rolled his eyes. "Relax, Mr. Diaz, I knew he wouldn't actually do it."

"I don't want to tell another man his own business," Burke said. "But if someone went and did that to me, I'd lay him out—hard."

"That's the difference between people like you and people like us," Dardner replied. "We're educated. You're not. We know how to settle—"

When Amos's fist smashed into Dardner's nose it sounded like a wet rag being thrown against the wall. The force of the blow sent Dardner flying. He rolled backwards and crashed into the bottom of a bookshelf. Amos winced as he massaged his knuckles. Burke clapped his hands together and whistled.

"Damn, who knew you packed that kind of punch? You did just like I said—laid that mouthy shit out HARD."

Julia knelt beside Dardner. "Is he okay?" Amos asked her.

Dardner pushed Julia away. "I'm fine." He got up on unsteady legs while using the bookshelf to brace himself. Two lines of dark blood ran parallel from the bottom of his nose to his upper lip. "It appears I was wrong, Mr. Diaz. You're not an educated man. You're an animal—the same as him. I look forward to making that very clear in my report to the authorities. Everything that you were and anything that you ever hoped to be will be over after today. That's my promise to you, and rest assured, I intend to keep it."

"Yeah?" Amos said with a shrug. "Fine. I don't care. Keep talking and I'm going to knock your ass out again. That's my promise to you, and rest assured, I intend to keep it. Now sit down and shut up."

Dardner opened his mouth to say something more. Amos gave him a hard, "this is not the time to be fucking with me" stare. Dardner's mouth promptly closed. He returned to his chair and wiped away the blood under his nose with the already bloodied sleeve of his jacket.

"Where'd you learn to hit like that?" Burke asked.

Amos was still rubbing his knuckles. "My grandfather was a boxer for the Castro government in Cuba before his family escaped to the United States. He taught me when I was a boy. I guess I never forgot. That's the first punch I've thrown in a very long time."

"Well, you sure as hell made it a good one," Burke said while sliding the Glock into the front of his pants. "Makes me wonder if I could handle you one on one."

Amos locked eyes with Burke. "I hope we don't have to find out."

"Me too, Mr. Diaz."

Amos took out his phone, read a text, then looked up. "The pizza is ready," he said. "They'll leave it in the courtyard in just a few minutes. Should I be the one to go get it?"

"No," Burke answered. "Let Julia do it. The rest of us will wait here until she comes back."

"You trust me?" Julia said.

"Yeah, I do. If anyone asks why you'd come back, tell them it's because I'll start shooting the other two if you don't."

"Would you?"

"Just come back and we won't have to worry about it."

"I will. I promise."

Burk smiled. "I know. I'll be waiting."

Julia went to the exit door, put her hand on it, and then turned around. All three men were watching her.

She pushed open the door and walked into the

courtyard.

CHAPTER 24

4:27 p.m.

"Don't move. Stay right there."

Julia stopped and put her hands up and then watched Markley walk toward her with a pizza box in his hands. "Are you okay?" he asked.

Julia nodded. "I'm fine. Just here for the pie." That's when she noted the three red dots on her chest.

"The feds have snipers on the roof," Markley said. "Don't make any sudden movement." He handed her the pizza and looked toward the library. "What's going on in there?"

"We're talking is all. Everything's fine."

"Talking?"

"Yeah, just talking. Amos seems to think Mr. Burke is very close to letting us all go."

"So, you're not in any danger?"

"Immediate danger? No, I don't think so."

Markley took another step toward Julia, so the red sniper dots were on his back instead of her chest. "Ms. Hodson, can you tell me how many weapons he has?"

"There's just a handgun. The rifles his sons had weren't loaded."

"Really? You're absolutely sure about that?"

"Yes—100%. Now can you tell me something?"

"What's that?"

"This pizza, did you do something to it?"

"What do you mean?"

"I mean, did you put drugs in it or something? Will it knock us out if we eat it?"

Markley shook his head. "No, it's just a pizza. A few suggested we lace it with something, but that idea was dropped. They couldn't be certain it might not cause an overdose. If it was only Burke eating it, they wouldn't have cared, but we assumed everyone was having some."

"Yeah, we're all pretty hungry. I should probably get back." Julia cocked her head. "Are people chanting in the parking lot?"

"It's getting worse out there. The road into the school is choked with vehicles. Lines of people are marching in. A bunch of them are ex-military."

"Ex-military? Why?"

"You didn't know? Burke personally saved nine soldiers over in Iraq after an IED attack left them all stranded on a road forty miles outside Baghdad. It was a four-hour firefight. Burke held his ground and kept the enemy away until help arrived. He was awarded the Silver Star for it."

"Willy Burke is a war hero?"

"He was a hero," Markley said. "Now he's just some whack-job who took a school hostage."

"He's not crazy. He just wants to be heard. Are his sons okay?"

Markley shrugged. "Last I heard they're fine. They

were taken to the county juvenile detention center about an hour ago. I'm not sure how long they'll be made to stay there. Word is the Feds want to charge Walter as an adult."

"That's awful."

"No, Ms. Hodson, that's reality. They did a very bad thing. You say Mr. Burke wants to be heard. Fine, who doesn't? But that doesn't give anyone the right to take over a school."

"We all make mistakes."

"Sure, but this was a doozy."

The sound of cheers carried into the courtyard. Markley hung his head. "Goddammit, I just want this thing to be over before someone gets hurt." He looked up. "I sure hope Mr. Diaz is right about Burke being ready to end this and come out."

"I guess we'll know soon."

"Unless it's right now, that won't be soon enough."

"Hang in there, Officer Markley."

"I should be telling you that, Ms. Hodson."

"I'm pretty sure you just did."

Julia turned around and walked back to the library. The smell of melted cheese, cured meats, and tomato sauce wafted up from the pizza box. Burke smiled when he saw her. Julia smiled back. Amos took the box, opened the lid, and set it on a chair. "Everyone eat up," he said.

Soon, the pizza was gone. Even Dardner had a slice. Burke sat down and stretched his legs out in front of him. "That was good," he said. "You talk to anyone out there?"

Julia nodded. "Officer Markley, the school resource

officer. He was alone. Well, except for the snipers on the roof, but I couldn't see them. He told me something about you, Mr. Burke."

"Don't believe it. People like him have been lying about people like me for a long time."

"He said you were a hero."

Burke looked down. "Oh."

"You saved the lives of nine other men."

Burke's voice sounded as far away as the memory he was reliving. "Yeah, I suppose."

"He also said there's a bunch of ex-military out in the parking lot. They came here to show their support. They came here for you."

Burke looked up with eyes wet with tears. "Really?"

"Yes. There's a line of people trying to get here, and they all want to see this end safely for everyone."

Amos put the phone on the floor. "It's your words, Mr. Burke. I told you—they have meaning. They matter. You matter. Should we continue?"

"No," Burke said with a shake of his head. "It's your turn, Mr. Diaz. What's your part in all this? Why are you trying to help me?"

Dardner leaned forward. "Yes, go ahead and explain yourself. I'm certain the Feds would like to hear your version as well."

"This isn't about me," Amos replied. "This is about all of us."

Burke pointed at the phone. "You, me, us, whatever. It's your turn to talk so start talking."

"About what?"

"About whatever you think you need to get off

your chest," Burke replied. "I spoke plenty already and talking isn't my thing. You're a teacher. You should have a whole shit-ton to say to the people out there."

"What if all I have to say is that it's time for us to go home? You heard Julia. They have snipers positioned on the roof. The only way this ends well is for you to give up."

"Huh? It was your idea to talk and now you've got nothing to say?"

Dardner smirked. "Because he's a coward. Mr. Diaz wanted to use you for whatever sick game this is. He won't speak up now because that would make him undeniably complicit. You're going to jail, Mr. Burke, but so will he. You'll both have plenty of time to do all the talking you want when you're there."

Amos looked at Julia. She nodded. He turned to Burke. "I get to say what I want? You won't fly off the handle if I say something you don't like?"

"Yeah," Burke said. "Do your thing. Speak your mind. How's that poem go? 'Rage against the dying of the light' or something? Well, rage on, Mr. Diaz. I'm far from the angriest one here. That would be you. Get it all out. I want to hear it."

Amos pulled the phone toward him. "Okay, you get extra credit for the Dylan Thomas reference. I'll do it." He turned the intercom system on, gave Julia another look, and then began.

"This is Mr. Amos Diaz. I'm a teacher here at Sky Valley High. I first want to ask that everyone in the parking lot listening right now to please do so with respect for those around you. Violence solves nothing.

It isn't the answer. Some of us disagree strongly with others. That's fine. That's life. Let us not lose sight of our shared humanity to lesser emotion and resulting conflict. We must be better than that.

"Mr. Burke has been kind enough to offer me this opportunity to speak. He has been nothing less than a gracious host under extraordinarily difficult circumstances. As I already told someone earlier, while what Mr. Burke did today was wrong, I understand the motivation to want to be heard. He's a flawed man but a good one. I hope the authorities keep that in mind when this situation is finally, and peacefully, concluded.

"I'm going to start my comments with an admission. It's a subject I actually shared with a colleague earlier today and one I would like to try and expand upon with all of you now. I've thought about death a great deal lately. So much so there are days it seems I hardly have time to think of anything else. I used to fear death. That was back when I was a younger man still fooled by the hope of supposed possibility before the grinding routine of real life intervened and snatched those dreams away and stomped them into oblivion. Now I think death might not be so bad.

"I know I'm not the only one. Call it depression, anxiety, terminal unhappiness with how so little of my life turned out the way I thought it would, my story is legion. It's like how after a particularly long and hard day, you welcome sleep. You just want to close your eyes and disappear from this world. To quiet the taunting whispers in your own head. Yes, it's like that but also with the hope that I never wake up. That this time when sleep takes me, it won't ever let go.

"You see, I don't feel much anymore. And what is left for me to feel is sadness, regret, disappointment, and shame. After weeks and months and years of feeling just those things, is it any surprise when you come to a place in your life where you hope not to feel anything at all ever again?

"Not so long ago, I realized I have fewer days ahead of me than days behind me. That realization was like a cold hard slap to the face, and every day that ends, the sting gets worse. It's not so much the passing of time that bothers me as it is the realization I've experienced so little true happiness during this thing that is my life. The people I've known, those few I allowed in, ultimately left me disappointed and confirmed that I am and will always be alone.

"Think about it. How much living do we actually do while we're alive? I say very little. We exist, we survive, but we're not truly living, are we? Life is a deadly routine. Do you notice how the older you become, the harder it is to decipher the differences between one month and the next? It's all mortgage payments, television programs, and grocery lists. The winters get longer and the summers shorter. This goes on and on until entire years become blurs of indifferent existence. Why care? Why bother? Why keep trying to do and be better? None of it really matters. It never did, and it never will.

"Even sex becomes an inconvenient distraction at best but more likely a source of ongoing disappointment until it's something to be avoided altogether. As for love, forget it. Love is a myth. A hoax. The cruelest of manipulators. And yet, what is life without love? Is such a life worth living? No. No it is not. And there you have it. The uncomfortable answer to my dark dilemma. To be or not to be. That really is the question, isn't it? It's the one that keeps me up at night when all I want to do is have a few uninterrupted hours of sleep.

"Which brings me to Mr. Burke. I understand his frustration because in so many ways, it's my own. I understand it, I appreciate it, and I respect it, even if I also happen to disagree with his method of expression. We're already dead, aren't we? The other day, there was a woman standing in line with me at a check-out counter. She smiled but her eyes said something very different. I saw in them the same pain and regret and hopelessness I feel. I see that look from people all the time. It's everywhere around us, yet so too is all the pretending that's there to convince ourselves it'll be okay. The forced laughter. The media distractions. The constant texting with all those words that say absolutely nothing—at least not anything real. We were never meant to have to give and take so much phoniness. It's debilitating to the point of making emotional cripples of us all.

"And these places we call schools? They're among the worst offenders of all. They beat phoniness into the kids until those kids forget what sincerity ever really felt like. Superficial emotion takes precedence over facts, and then we have the audacity to ask ourselves why school shootings take place. We create monsters who cannot fathom a world in which their fake feelings don't matter. Who watch the world on a phone screen while it slowly but steadily pulls them away from the real world all around them. And it's not just the kids. I see parents and teachers doing the same thing. There are so few left who are really paying attention, and we are all suffering for it.

"William Burke showed up to this school today because he had a message. Agree or disagree with that message, it doesn't really matter. The media will portray him as an angry man who did a terrible thing. We all know that. It's what the media does. And yet, I'll remind all of you that no one was hurt. Frightened yes, but not hurt. The weapons he brought were not loaded. They were harmless, simply tools to get our attention. I will tell you something you might not know. I am confident Mr. Burke actually saved lives today, either in the here and now or the then and there. I won't say how I know this because, well, that's my own business. He saved my life, of that I'm sure. I repeat, Willy Burke saved my life today. Please remember that when we finally walk out of here. He will no doubt be punished for what he did at this school. He should also be rewarded."

Amos turned off the intercom. When he looked up, he found three faces staring back at him. "What?" he said.

Julia stood. "We need to talk—now. In the office."

Burke got up as well and extended his hand. He told Amos thank you as the two men shook.

"Thanks for what?" Amos asked him.

"For trying to see my side of things. I haven't had much of that from anyone for a very long time."

Julia was on the move. She turned around and motioned for Amos to follow. Burke leaned in close. "You in trouble?" he whispered.

"I'm not sure," Amos replied.

"Looks like she means business."

"Yeah, I'd say so."

Amos went into the office. Julia closed the door behind him. When he turned around, she was staring at him intensely. "What?" he said.

"Don't you dare 'what me' again, Mr. Diaz. I asked you earlier today why you brought a gun to school. Now I know."

"You do?"

"We're not going to talk about it. Not here. Not now. Not ever."

"Really? Then why'd you tell me to follow you in here?"

"Because I want you to know I'll keep my mouth shut but only if you do something."

"What's that?"

"Get out of teaching and don't look back. It's killing you, Amos. I knew you were unhappy. You already made that clear to me, but I didn't know how deep that unhappiness went. You need to get as far away as possible from all of this. It's turning you into something scary, something dangerous."

"I'll be fine."

"No, you won't. I really don't want to have to say it. The gun, your state of mind, the words you just said publicly. I'm not stupid. Don't treat me like I am. You're an angry, violent man. I can't allow you to go back into a classroom. I won't. You need help, and then you need to find something else to do."

"Julia, what are you saying?"

"I'm saying you're done as a teacher, but I would really rather you make that choice for yourself. Right here and now. Otherwise..."

Julia's voice trailed off. Amos lifted his head and straightened his shoulders. "Otherwise you'll make it for me. Is that what you're telling me?"

"Yes."

"I see."

"I hope you do because I really mean it. You're never going to step foot in a classroom again. I won't let you."

"You're really serious about this, aren't you?"

"I am. Don't make me be the one to stop you, Amos. Walk away from it on your own. There has to be something else you'd like to do. Somewhere you'd rather be. Can you think of a place or a time when you were truly happy? If so, then that's where you need to try and get back to."

"I never wanted to hurt anyone. Not really."

"I know that, but I also know there's something in you that's not right, and this job is making it worse. The sooner you quit teaching, the sooner you can return to being a human being."

"Do you remember Bill Huck?"

Julia nodded. "I do. He taught science, right?"

"Yes, for 30 years. He hated it. He was always griping, always counting down the days when he could retire with a full pension. The only time I would see him smile was when he was talking about the boat he was restoring. It was some old thing he bought for next to nothing at an auction. He worked on it year after year after year. Kept a map of the coast in his classroom with a bunch of inlets circled in red ink. Old Bill would point to them and say he was going to spend the rest of his life visiting every single one. From Alaska to the Gulf of Mexico, he would see them all."

"Bill died. I went to the funeral."

"Yeah, five months after he retired, he dropped dead of a massive heart attack. That boat of his never saw the water and neither did Bill, and all that dreaming over all those years about visiting far-off places died with him. He wasn't really missed around here. It's like I said, Bill wasn't much for friendly chatter. When he did say something, it was usually to complain about this job he despised so much. But he and I did speak about the water and being on a boat. I spent summers in Florida with my grandfather and he had this little skiff with an old, smoky two-stroke that he let me take anywhere I wanted. I must have spent a thousand hours on that thing driving it way too fast and hitting the waves so hard it felt like my teeth would rattle right out of my skull. The drone of the motor, the smell of gasoline and oil, the slap of the water against the hull—it was so beautiful and so perfect. From morning to night, I explored and fished every nook and cranny of the Intercoastal Waterway that was within a hundred miles of my grandfather's home. The things I saw, the freedom—oh, the freedom—it seems so long ago, so impossible now, that part of me wonders if it ever really happened at all. I really don't think I was made for this time, Julia.

I'm so out of place here. I don't belong. I never have. I know that. I've always known it and perhaps that is the true source of the anger and frustration you say you sense in me. The last time I felt like I belonged, when I was truly where I was meant to be, was during those summers on the water. I've never felt that way again, and I fear I never will."

"Amos, look at me." Julia took hold of Amos's hands and pulled him toward her. "Just go. Don't wait. Don't make excuses. Don't talk yourself out of it. Sell your home, cash out your retirement, and go find that boy you used to be before he's gone forever. Don't let the light inside of you go out completely."

"You mean early retirement?"

"Quit, resign, early retirement, whatever you want to call it doesn't matter. Just do it, Amos. Get out of here. Find the water. Find yourself. Find happiness. Hell, maybe you'll find love. But whatever you do, don't settle. Don't make excuses. Don't put it off. Don't became another Bill Huck."

"You could come with me."

Julia shook her head. "No, Amos, I can't. This is your journey not mine. I enjoy teaching and as flawed as it might be, I like my life here. Some people do best when they're alone. Maybe you're one of them."

"We're all together alone, screaming in silence," Amos said with a pained smile.

"Where's that from?"

"A novel titled Manitoba by an author named Decklan Stone. I read it over a weekend laying under the sun on a beautiful, isolated beach in Whaleback Key the summer before my seventeenth birthday. I'd forgotten all about it until just now. Makes me want to read it again. I bet I still have a copy of it somewhere at home."

"You should," Julia said. "You want to know why?"

"I think you're about to tell me."

"Because right now, while you were telling me about that book and that weekend, you were smiling. I mean really smiling, Amos. I don't think I've ever seen you do that before."

Amos frowned. "I'm pretty sure I wasn't smiling."

"Not with your mouth—your eyes. That light hasn't gone out in you quite yet. It's still there."

"Maybe, just maybe, a person really can go back to something better."

"It's worth a try."

Amos pulled Julia close and hugged her tight. After a moment's hesitation, she hugged him back. "Thank you," he whispered into her ear.

"For what?" she asked.

"For understanding. For everything."

CHAPTER 25

5:12 p.m.

Burke handed Amos the Glock. "I believe this is yours," he said. "I was thinking maybe it's time we call it a day. I'm ready to walk out there and take my lumps. I won't tell anyone I took it from you. As far as I'm concerned, that never happened. Hopefully, that'll minimize any damage the cops might try to send your way."

"I don't know if that'll help much at this point, but I appreciate the gesture, Mr. Burke."

"Not a problem, Mr. Diaz."

Dardner got up. "Bullshit. I'm telling them everything. The two of you are peas from the same pod, and you're both going down for what happened today."

"Shut up, Doyle," Julia said. "The only thing you're going to say about Amos is that he did everything he could to keep us safe."

"The hell I will."

Julia went up to Dardner and poked his chest. "The hell you won't. For once in your life, stop trying to make yourself bigger by making other people smaller."

Dardner bent down until his nose nearly touched Julia's forehead. "I don't need you telling me what to say about anything. This time next week, if you're lucky, you'll be back to drawing your little pictures for the students."

"Fine, you want to complain to the authorities about Mr. Diaz? I'll go to the school board about your workplace sexcapades. There'll be lots of questions, an investigation, the media will be all over it."

Dardner's eyes darted from side to side as he stepped back. "I have no idea what you're referring to, and I won't be intimidated by empty threats."

"An empty threat? Really? That's your defense? You think your wife will see it that way? Perhaps she'd like to discuss it with Ronda. How many times did you sneak in here to use her for a quickie? And don't think for a second that isn't exactly what you did—use her. If she was a stronger woman, she would have already called you out for what you did. Then again, if she was a stronger woman, she never would have let you touch her in the first place."

"I thought you two were friends. Why would you cause her so much pain by making these accusations public?"

"So, you admit to the affair?"

Dardner's confident smirk let the others know he had no fear of Julia's threats. "I admit nothing. What may or may not have taken place between consenting adults is no business of the school board or anyone else. Willfully spreading rumors against other staff though? That would lay the groundwork for potential dismissal. Be very careful how you proceed, Ms. Hodson. However inconsequential your role is here at the school, I would hate to see it come to an abrupt and embarrassing end. Know your place—and stay there."

"You are such an asshole."

"Perhaps I am, but you would do well to remember that I'm also the one in charge. Now get out of my way. I'm leaving."

Amos held up the hand that wasn't holding the Glock. "Wait. I need to let Markley know we're coming out. You go walking out there alone unannounced and you're just as apt to get shot."

"Fine by me," Julia said just loud enough for Dardner to hear.

"Very well, Mr. Diaz, let them know. I'll be leading the way of course."

Amos went into the office and made the call. Markley picked up on the first ring. "Thank God," he said when Amos told him they were getting ready to leave the library. "We need to end this now before it spirals out of control. The anti-gun crowd is screaming at the pro-gun crowd, and sooner or later, somebody is going to do something really stupid and people are going to get hurt. Are you on your way out now?"

"Yes," Amos answered. "We should be stepping through the front door in just a few minutes."

"Okay, we'll get everyone back as best we can. Make sure you all have your hands up where they can be seen. Stay in a group close together. Leave the weapons in the library and please make sure Mr.

Burke knows there is to be no resistance of any kind. The agents out here are in no mood to put up with any nonsense. He'll be cuffed as soon as he's secured and then transported out of here, so we can hopefully get everyone else to go back home and give us our school back. Does anyone need any medical attention?"

"No, we're all still fine."

"Alright. I'll see you very soon."

Amos put his phone away and joined the others. "They're ready for us. Mr. Burke, you're going to be arrested as soon as you're outside the school. Officer Markley wants to make sure you don't intend to resist. It's for your safety as much as anyone else's."

"Shit, I won't do nothing," Burke replied. "Let's get this over with."

The group turned as one toward the door—except for Burke. "Hold on," he said. "I want to tell you all something before we leave."

Dardner sighed. His hand was already on the door. "We don't have time for speeches. I'll lead. You follow."

"Go ahead, Mr. Burke," Amos said. "Tell us what's on your mind."

Burke shifted on his feet and cleared his throat. "Well, I know what I did was wrong and there's gonna be a price to pay. That said, I'm not so sure I'd do it any different even if I could. And that's because of you, Mr. Diaz, and you, Ms. Hodson. Maybe we're friends now, and maybe we're not, but I'd like to think so. I don't really have friends. At least not the kind a man can trust. Outside of my boys, I don't have much of anything. I just wanted to let you know and tell you thanks before I get hauled away."

"You're going to be fine, William," Julia replied with a tight-lipped smile as she lightly gripped Burke's arm. "This too shall pass, and you'll have your life back. We all will."

Dardner nodded. "Yeah, it'll pass all right. After he rots in a cell for the next twenty years. Now let's go. I have a school to run."

Burke grunted and shook his head. "I have to give it to you, Mr. Principal. You don't ever stop thinking your shit don't stink. Even after a hard smack or two, that mouth of yours just keeps on slicing and dicing. Suppose I gotta respect that, as much as I'd like nothing more right now than to make a hard fist and give it another crack."

"Oh, you'd like that wouldn't you? Well go ahead then. Add another year or two to the prison sentence I'm sure is coming your way."

"That's enough," Amos said. "Let's go."

Dardner rose up to his full height and put his hand on the door. "Yes, let's go. Follow me."

The courtyard was empty. Amos reminded the others to walk slowly and stick together. They heard a chorus of shouting coming from the parking lot at the front of the school. Dardner strode confidently toward the main entrance. He ordered the others to keep up.

Police officers shouted for people to get back and make way.

"My God," Julia whispered. "Look at all of them."

A thousand faces watched and waited for the doors to open. The lights from a line of police vehicles bathed the surrounding concrete and asphalt in swirling blankets of blue and red. Dardner stopped in front of the double doors. His face was tight. His eyes blinked each time a blast of light hit them.

"What are you waiting for, Mr. Principal?" Burke asked.

Dardner ran a hand over the thin strands of hair that partially covered his scalp, straightened his jacket, and gripped the door handle. "Here we go," he said.

For a few long seconds, the parking lot went still. No one shouted. Nothing moved. Even the lights seemed to pause and wait.

Dardner put his hands up, smiled, and stepped outside. "We're okay. I have Mr. Burke with me. He's ready to give himself up. Please let us through."

A line of armed officers ordered the people to stay back and keep the path to the parking lot clear. A helicopter hovered above, pummeling the area with blasts of wind.

Markley emerged from the throng and motioned for the others to follow. "Right this way. We're going to get you all out of here."

Two FBI agents stepped out from behind Markley and pointed their weapons at Burke. "He's unarmed," Dardner assured them, talking as if he was in charge of the entire operation.

Burke stopped and allowed himself to be handcuffed. "Take it easy," he said grimacing. "I'm not going anywhere."

Dardner raised his hands even higher over his head while he addressed the swirling mass of people. "See? Everything is going to be fine. On behalf of the district, I want to thank you all for your support and to let you know I'm very much looking forward to getting back to work serving the students, parents, and staff of this wonderful school."

A woman shouted Dardner's name. Burke broke free from the FBI agents and lunged forward. "Dardner, get down!" he yelled.

There was a flash, two loud pops, followed by screams of shock and terror. Dardner cried out as Burke collapsed a few feet in front of him. A mass of police officers pounced on the female shooter, disarmed her, and took her away as she continued to wail Dardner's name.

"No-no-no," Julia whimpered. "It was Ronda. Ronda shot him." Both she and Amos scrambled to where Burke lay in a growing pool of his own blood. He was on his side, twisted like a broken doll, with his hands cuffed behind him. He looked up with eyes full of confusion, pain, and fear. Two dark wet circles stained the front of his shirt. His fingers curled inward and scratched at the concrete underneath him.

"I'm right here, William," Julia said. "I'm holding your hand."

"Oh, hey there," he replied. "I guess I forgot to duck."

Markley knelt down next to Burke and yelled for the medics. When he saw the gunshot wounds in Burke's chest his face went white. "Fucking hell. Why would Ms. Moore do that? She's the goddamn librarian." He glanced at Dardner. "I know what I saw. She was aiming for you not Burke."

Dardner stared at the ground. Nothing of the

haughty arrogance he had displayed seconds earlier remained. Without saying anything more, he turned and walked away.

Burke's body spasmed. "Is he safe?" he croaked. "Is Mr. Principal okay?"

"Yeah, he's fine," Amos answered. "You saved the worthless son-of-a-bitch."

Burke's smile looked more like a hideous snarl as it revealed teeth soaked in blood. "Okay. I did a good thing, right?"

"You did a very good thing," Julia said as tears left moist tracks down both her cheeks.

Burke closed his eyes tight and groaned. "I've watched men at their end say how cold dying feels. Had no idea how right they were. It's the kind of cold that burns. Please let my boys know. Let them know what I done. That in the end, I tried to make it right."

Julia tightened her grip around Burke's hand. "You're going to tell them yourself, William. Do you hear me? William?"

Burke didn't answer. Julia shook her head and scowled. "No, this isn't right. This can't happen. Say it, Amos. Say this can't happen."

"I wish I could, Julia. God, how I wish I could."

Willy Burke's eyes suddenly opened as he stared up at the early evening sky—or perhaps something beyond that sky that only he could see. His mouth fell open. He grimaced, squeezed Julia's hand tight, and sighed. "Wow," he whispered.

The medical team arrived, pushed everyone back, and took Burke away. Agent Torrance introduced herself to Amos and Julia and then informed them it was going to be a long night of statements and interviews with local, state, and federal law enforcement. The school district's attorney intervened at that point and informed Torrance all district employees would cooperate fully at the appropriate time—and no sooner than tomorrow. Torrance reluctantly withdrew, as did most everyone else. People returned to their vehicles. The parking lot's lights came on, illuminating the pavement and crime scene tape in a soft white glow.

Amos and Julia didn't move for nearly an hour. They watched in silence as law enforcement continued to scurry into and out of the school until finally, they too were gone.

"What's going to happen to Ronda?"

"I don't know," Amos answered. "Hopefully, she'll get the help she needs. Her days working as a librarian are definitely over."

"I feel guilty."

"Why is that?"

"If she had shot Doyle like she wanted to, if she had killed him, I don't think I would have cared. In fact, I think I would have liked it. That scares the hell out of me, Amos. It's like there's a part of me I don't even know—this monster living in my head just waiting for a chance to come out and take over."

"I know exactly what you mean."

"You do?"

"Yeah, I do."

Julia looked up at Amos for a long time before she spoke again. "Are you ever going to tell me the truth about why you really brought that gun to school today?"

Amos breathed deep and stared straight ahead. "I don't need to tell you because you already know. Besides, whatever that truth might have been, it doesn't matter. Everything is different now—especially me."

A shooting star flashed across the night sky. Amos followed its ethereal arc, and then, like so much else in his world, it was gone.

"What does a teacher do after an especially difficult day at work?"

Julia's brows drew down together. "What?"

"They go home. Goodnight, Ms. Hodson."

Julia watched Amos walk across the parking lot to his car. He seemed smaller, frailer, lost. She waited for him to turn around.

He never did.

He was there.

And then he was gone.

CHAPTER 26

Three years later.
Cayo Verde, Cuba.

A mos didn't mind the stifling afternoon heat and humidity. Freedom, real freedom, felt good regardless the weather. He stretched out his legs and dug his sunbaked toes into the pristine white sands of the sparsely populated beach that was his new home. Tourists came and went, but they were few, while the locals worked and played at a pace that was both leisurely and dignified.

Deep laugh lines shot out from the corners of his eyes and down the sides of his mouth. Amos had laughed more in the last sixteen months than he could recall laughing his entire life before returning to the place that was his true beginning.

He wore his white cotton shirt open, exposing a chest that was leaner and more defined than it had been in a very long time. His dark arms were sinewy-strong, the hands rough and calloused from the early morning ritual of checking his fishing nets. It was real work. The kind that often left him sore and tired. He loved it.

If he didn't catch enough to sell at the local

market, Amos always caught just enough to help feed himself and the few neighbors around him he happily counted as friends. That's how it was in Cayo Verde. Everyone watched out for everyone else, especially those like Amos who were descended from families who had lost everything decades ago to the authoritarian Castro regime.

The little bit of inlet beach Amos lay upon, its rickety dock and weathered shack, was where his grandfather had been born and lived during his youth. Before Castro, three Diaz generations had called it home. The land records confirmed this. The newly formed Cuban government did for Amos what it was doing for other displaced Cuban progeny: allowing them a chance to reclaim their rightful inheritance.

Amos reached into the small ice chest next to him and grabbed a beer. He stared out at the breeze-blown blue water and noted a collection of dark clouds in the distance that hinted of possible rain later that evening. He opened the beer, took a sip, and closed his eyes. Cold beer had never tasted so good before as it did in Cuba. Amos kept his eyes shut, breathed deep, and smiled. The air smelled of sea salt, sand, and mango from the cluster of two-hundred-year-old fruit trees that grew near the side of the shack.

It was the smell of happiness, contentment, and of life once again worth living.

"Hello, Mr. Diaz."

Amos had to squint because of the sun but already knew the voice and the face it belonged to.

Willy Burke had accepted the open invitation to

visit him in Cuba. "Those pictures you sent to me in prison don't do it justice," he said. "My goodness it really is something. Like a goddamn postcard from paradise on earth."

"Hi, Amos. We finally made it." Julia's smile was as wide and warm as ever.

Amos put his beer down and got up. Burke cocked his head. "You look taller."

"Lost some weight," Amos replied while rubbing his exposed stomach.

"And you're so dark," Julia added.

"Yeah, well, we tend to get a lot of sun down here."

"I'll say."

The three went quiet. Seagulls cried out as waves gently licked the beach.

Burke suddenly stepped forward with open arms. "Come here, you black pirate bastard, and give me a hug." The embrace between the two men was as long as it was strong. When one started to pull away, the other held tight. Burke clapped Amos on the shoulders, looked into his dark eyes, and shook his head. "Check you out, Mr. Diaz. You're looking good— damn good."

Amos laughed. "Thanks."

"Where's my hug?" Julia asked.

Amos pulled her close and wrapped his arms around her. Like Burke, she didn't seem to want to let go. "It's so good to see you happy," she said. "You are happy, right?"

"Yeah, I really am. This place, everything about it—I can feel it in my bones. I wake up early and go to bed late because I don't want to waste a single minute more of this life. I love it. I love my life. Imagine that. C'mon, let me give you two the tour."

Amos showed them the sparse interior of the cabin, which was little more than a cot, a table and two chairs, a propane cooktop, an ancient fridge, and a bathroom closed off from the main room by a curtain. He explained how when it stormed, he loved standing in the open doorway and looking out at the angry waters and listening to the hiss of rain and wind. "And when the storm is over," he said, "there's this heavy-wet and warm smell to the air, like how I imagine the world was like when it was young. You know what I mean?"

Burke looked up at the cabin's cathedral ceiling where slivers of sunlight broke through small gaps in the rusted-out tin roof. "Yeah, I think I do. Kind of like everything washes away and starts over."

"Exactly," Amos said with a snap of his fingers. "That's it—like everything is starting over. That's the smell. That's the feeling I get."

Amos took them outside and knelt next to his modest vegetable garden that consisted of tomatoes, onions, corn, and cucumbers. "You can grow just about anything year-round here," he said while picking a couple of cherry tomatoes and then handing them to Julia and Burke. After plopping them into their mouths, they both remarked how they were the most delicious tomatoes they'd ever tasted.

"Oh, if you think that's good," Amos said, "you have to try a mango. It's a spiritual awakening. I promise."

Burke and Julia stood in stunned silence as they

watched Amos pull himself up into a mango tree and disappear into its dense, green branches. "I'll pick you out a prize winner," he yelled down to them. Seconds later, he dropped to the ground holding a beautiful red and yellow mango in one hand and a knife in the other. "Let me peel some of the skin back for you," he said before handing it to Julia. "Ladies first."

Julia bit deep and laughed hard when the fruit's juices ran down her chin. "Oh my gosh, it's so good." She handed the mango to Burke. "You have to try it."

Burke nodded as he chewed. "Can't get that in no supermarket, that's for sure. Even more impressive is how you climbed that tree. There's not a hint of teacher left in you."

"Ah," Amos said. "You haven't seen the boat. C'mon, it's right over here."

The dock was old, but the boat tied to it was nearly new. Amos ran a hand along its white bow. "She's a Grady White. Twin outboards, full fishing platform, head and sleeping quarters; it'll do thirty-five knots easy and push fifty if I need it to. I can get to Key West and back in less than a day. I've been to the Bahamas, Turks and Caicos, Haiti, Jamaica, the Cayman Islands, and plan to make a trip to Belize next summer. Some of those trips require I bring extra fuel, of course."

Julia arched her brows. "Oh, of course."

"Ms. Hodson, are you mocking my enthusiasm?"

"Why yes, Mr. Diaz, I most certainly am."

Later, as the sun gradually dipped below the ocean's limitless horizon, Julia sat in the sand bookended by Amos on one side and Burke on the other. Each of them nursed beers, shoeless and silent as they watched the last of the daylight give way to night. They had spent the day talking of the past. Burke spoke briefly of his time in prison and then spoke much more about the job he later obtained at a community resource center helping other war veterans transition back into civilian life.

"It's the kind of work that makes you realize that as bad as things might seem, there's always someone who has it a lot worse. I like it. I like helping people. It's given me a real sense of purpose."

Walter, his oldest, who had been granted supervision rights of Waylon while Burke was in prison, was now working full-time at an auto repair shop. Waylon was a junior at Sky Valley High and planned to join the military after graduation the following year.

"He's gonna be an MP," Burke said grinning. "Imagine that? A Burke boy wants to be a cop. Life sure can be funny when it's not kicking your ass."

Julia was still teaching art at the high school and planned to continue doing so for the foreseeable future. She also said it didn't hurt that Dardner had been forced into early retirement by the district. He wasn't missed by anyone on the staff. As for Ronda, she remained in a mental health facility since the shooting.

"I visited with her last month," Julia said. "She's doing okay. Feels terrible for what she did but is in no hurry to get out. She likes the routine and all the time she has for reading."

"And what about you two?" Amos asked. "Are we

talking a serious long-term situation here?"

Burke held his beer high. "Man, I hope so—if she'll have me."

The two clinked their bottles together and Julia smiled. "Play your cards right, Mr. Burke. Play your cards right."

The three grew quiet as the last of the beer was finished. Amos lay down with his arms behind his head. Burke and Julia glanced down at him and then did the same.

"Damn, look at all those stars," Burke said.

"And the sound of the waves," Julia added. "I could listen to that all night."

Burke let out a long, satisfied sigh. "What's the secret, Mr. Diaz?"

"Secret? To what?"

"Well, I was thinking something just now."

"Yeah?"

"I was thinking when I first saw you today sitting here all smiles and nods, it was like that little almost nonexistent sliver of happiness that used to be inside you—well, now it's all of you. You're the same but you're way different."

"Different how?"

"Different as in better. You got this gravitational pull thing happening around you now that makes it so when a person sees it, they want to be a part of it. I saw you and thought, there's a guy who's doing it right. There's a man living life on his own terms, and man I gotta say, it looks good. You're a goddamn miracle, Mr. Diaz. An inspiration. Back from the dead, reborn, whatever you want to call it—that's you."

Amos grunted. "I'm not the one who took two in the chest three years ago followed by a prison sentence. I'd have to give you the nod in the miracles department, Mr. Burke."

"Nah, all I did was survive. You're living and thriving. Big difference."

That seemed to make Amos stop and think. His mouth tightened as he looked up at the stars. "Maybe you're right. I guess. I don't know."

Julia sat up. "All these deep thoughts between you two has given me an idea."

Burke sat up as well. He was grinning like he already knew what Julia was thinking.

"What do you think, Mr. Diaz?" Julia held a joint between two fingers. "Care to join us?"

From further down the beach came the sound of children laughing. A dog barked. The smell of cooking meat was carried upon the wind. Amos propped himself up onto his elbows, looked at Julia and Burke, and rolled his eyes.

"Just like old times, huh?"

Julia lit up, inhaled, and shook her head. "No, not old times. These are better times. This is our time, together, right here and now." She passed the joint to Burke who took a hit.

"Damn right," Burke said. "We're the three amigos with our butts in the sand enjoying some Cuban-grown weed and beers under an ocean of stars. Life is fucking good."

Amos took the joint and shrugged. "I won't argue that. The man who has nothing has everything."

Burke pointed to the Grady White. "I'd say that

258

boat of yours is something."

Amos cracked a crooked grin. "True, but it allows me to break free of land and all the crap I've left behind: the house, the job, the pretending to care about things that don't really matter. That vessel tied to that old dock is a time machine. It takes me to places where the only thing that matters is what's right in front of me. I've been out in the big blue, miles from anything but for the first time in a very long time, seeing everything. All around me is water, sky, and the kind of silence that's so pure, so uninterrupted, so comforting, it's like going back to the womb. Time and obligation aren't nearly as important as just ...being. And that, my friends, is how life is meant to be lived. My only regret is that it took me so long to realize it."

"That's deep," Burke said right before he took another hit. "It's funny how you mention being miles from anything but seeing everything. I felt that very thing once. I'll never forget it as long as I live."

Julia and Amos both waited for Burke to continue. He pulled his knees close to his chest and wrapped his arms around them. "When I was on the ground after I was shot, I looked up and saw nothing and everything at the same time. Like the old saying about how a person's life flashes in front of them? It was like that, but it wasn't. I was a speck, a nothing, but also part of something more, like ripples from a tiny pebble dropped into the biggest goddamn glass of water you can possibly imagine. It was scary but amazing at the same time."

Amos scooped up some sand and rubbed it

between his fingers. "I remember that moment."

Burke turned his head. "You do?"

"There were a few seconds when you were looking right at me but didn't see me, like your eyes were fixated on something else. You said wow. You didn't sound afraid. More like pleasantly surprised."

"Pleasantly surprised," Burke whispered while staring out at the mirrorlike water. "Yeah, that sounds about right."

Amos got up and brushed the sand off his backside. "You two hungry?"

"I could eat something," Julia replied right before standing and then pulling Burke up with her.

"There's a little resort about a mile from here," Amos said. "They make a mighty fine ceviche. What do you think?"

Julia stood between Burke and Amos and put her arms around them. "I think I'm starving. Lead the way."

The three walked together along the water with only the moon to guide them until they spied the resort just beyond a bend in the beach where a finger of dark rock extended out into the watery gloom. Julia glanced up at Amos and smiled.

"What?" he said smiling back.

"Oh, I was just wondering how you might describe how much your life has changed. Like, in one word, what would it be?"

"Revenge."

"Revenge? Really?"

"Absolutely," Amos replied. "Revenge against the stupid, self-loathing, whiny little bitch that used to be me. Revenge against doing my life wrong for so long."

"That sounds like the makings of a great transformative story."

Burke nodded. "Yes indeed. Mr. Diaz's Revenge. I don't read much, but I'd sure as hell read that." He winked. "Especially if I was in it."

"Nah, I don't think anyone would be interested in a story about me."

Julia bumped Amos's side with her shoulder. "I wouldn't be so sure about that, Mr. Diaz."

The three kept walking, talking, and laughing together—each step, each word, each expression of friendship and love a new beginning.

Call it revenge. Call it whatever.

It felt good.

It felt right.

It felt like something worth living for.

Made in United States
Troutdale, OR
01/11/2024